T0338343

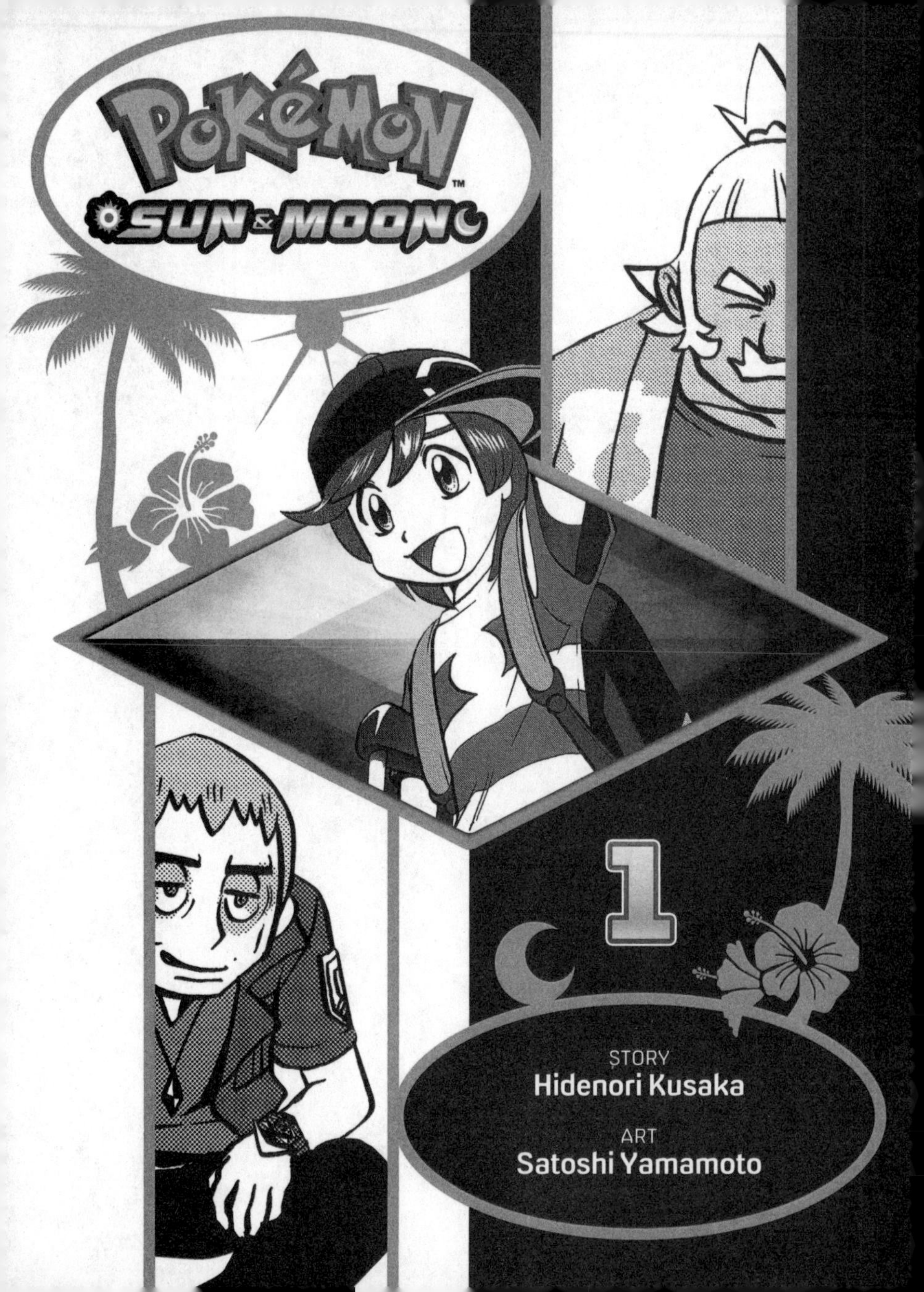

Pokémon™ Sun & Moon

1

STORY
Hidenori Kusaka

ART
Satoshi Yamamoto

Introduction

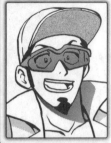

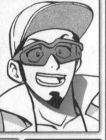

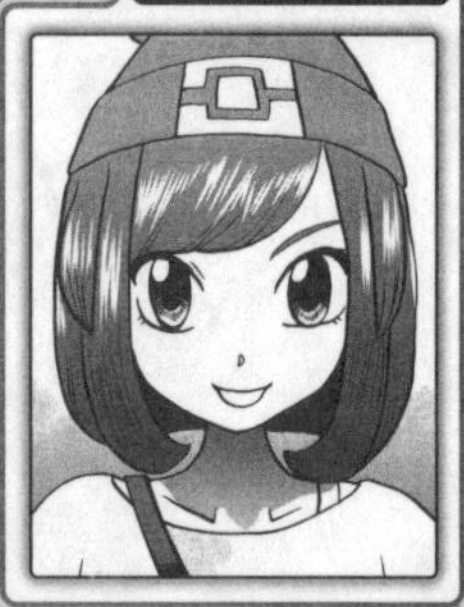

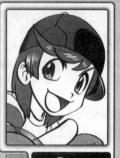

Sun

One of the main characters of this tale. A young Pokémon Trainer who makes a living doing all sorts of odd jobs, including working as a delivery boy. His dream is to save up a million dollars!

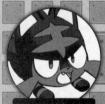

Moon

One of the main characters of this tale. A pharmacist who has traveled to Alola from a faraway region. She is a self-confident, original thinker. She is also an excellent archer.

Professor Kukui

A Pokémon researcher with a laboratory on Melemele Island. An expert on Pokémon moves who likes to experience them used against himself!

Dollar (Litten)

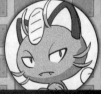

Cent (Alolan Meowth)

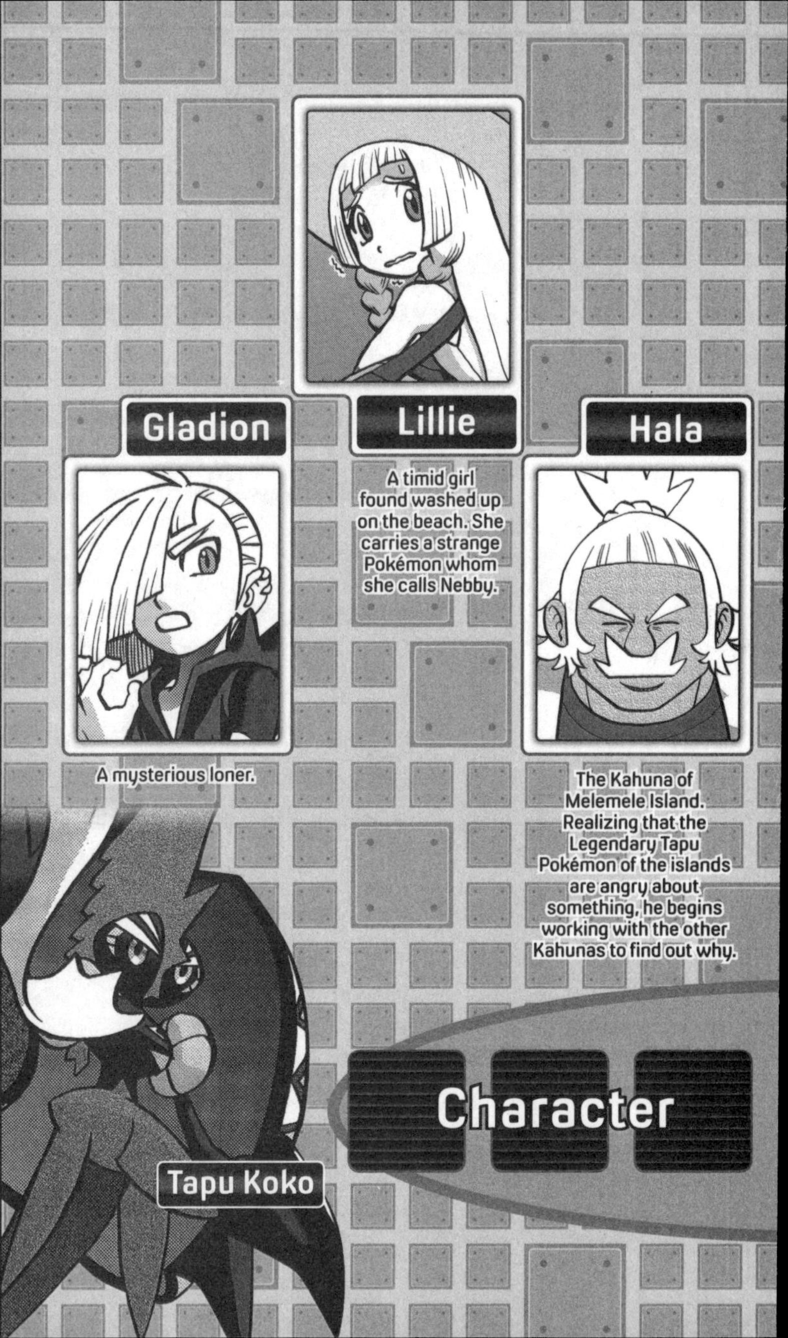
Character
Hala
The Kahuna of Melemele Island. Realizing that the Legendary Tapu Pokémon of the islands are angry about something, he begins working with the other Kahunas to find out why.
Lillie
A timid girl found washed up on the beach. She carries a strange Pokémon whom she calls Nebby.
Gladion
A mysterious loner.
Tapu Koko

CONTENTS

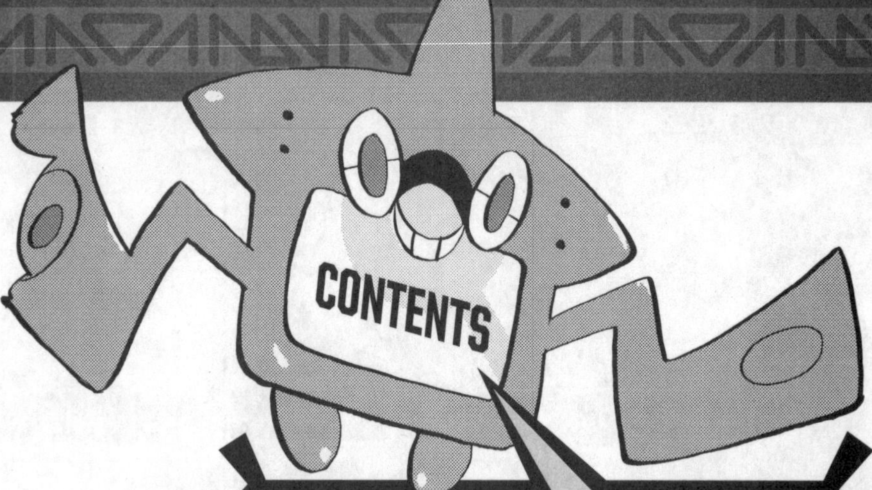

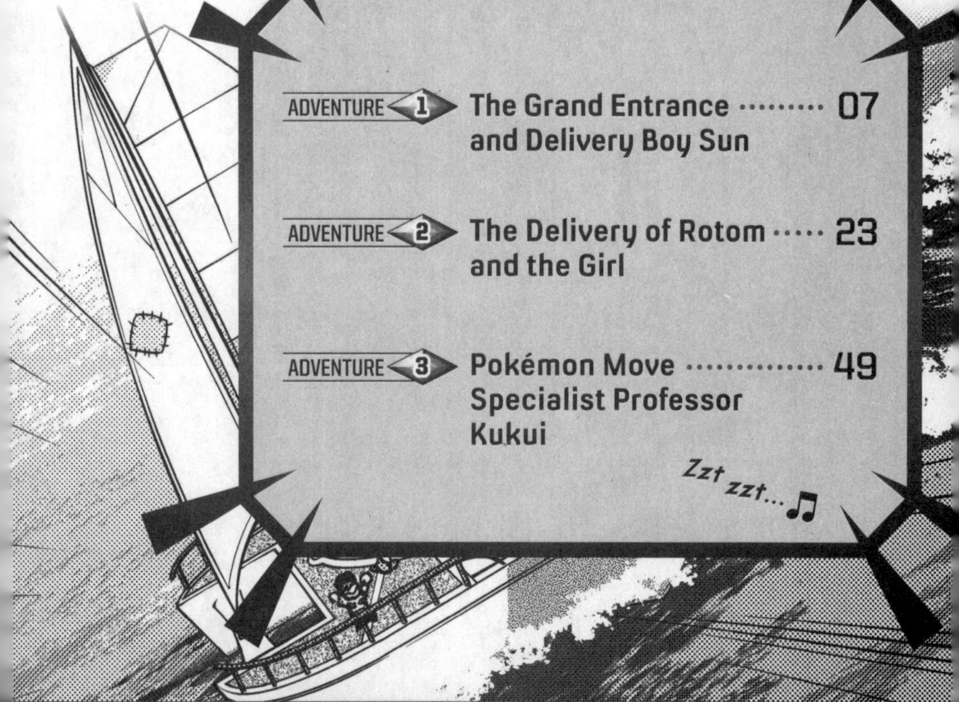
Zzt zzt...♫

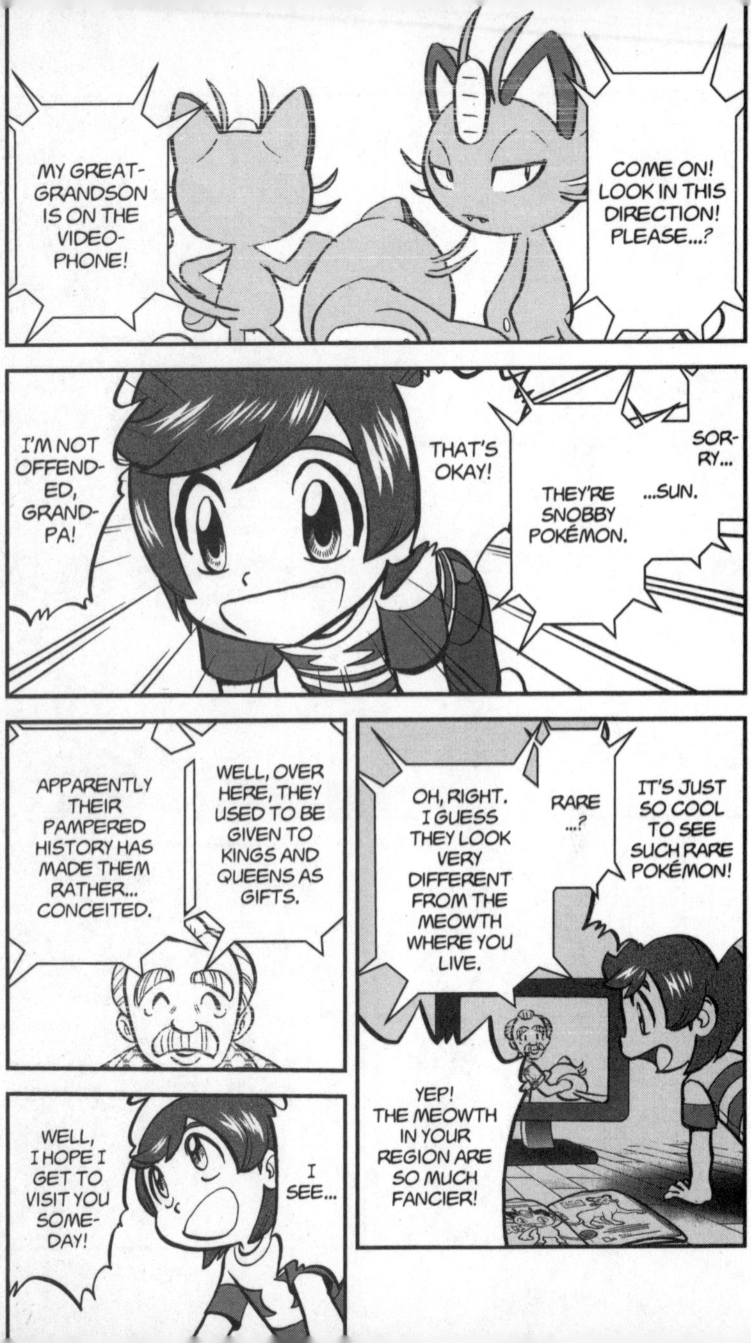
COME ON! LOOK IN THIS DIRECTION! PLEASE...?
MY GREAT-GRANDSON IS ON THE VIDEO-PHONE!
SORRY...
...SUN.
THEY'RE SNOBBY POKÉMON.
THAT'S OKAY!
I'M NOT OFFENDED, GRANDPA!
IT'S JUST SO COOL TO SEE SUCH RARE POKÉMON!
RARE...?
OH, RIGHT. I GUESS THEY LOOK VERY DIFFERENT FROM THE MEOWTH WHERE YOU LIVE.
YEP! THE MEOWTH IN YOUR REGION ARE SO MUCH FANCIER!
WELL, OVER HERE, THEY USED TO BE GIVEN TO KINGS AND QUEENS AS GIFTS.
APPARENTLY THEIR PAMPERED HISTORY HAS MADE THEM RATHER... CONCEITED.
I SEE...
WELL, I HOPE I GET TO VISIT YOU SOMEDAY!

Adventure 1
The Grand Entrance and Delivery Boy Sun

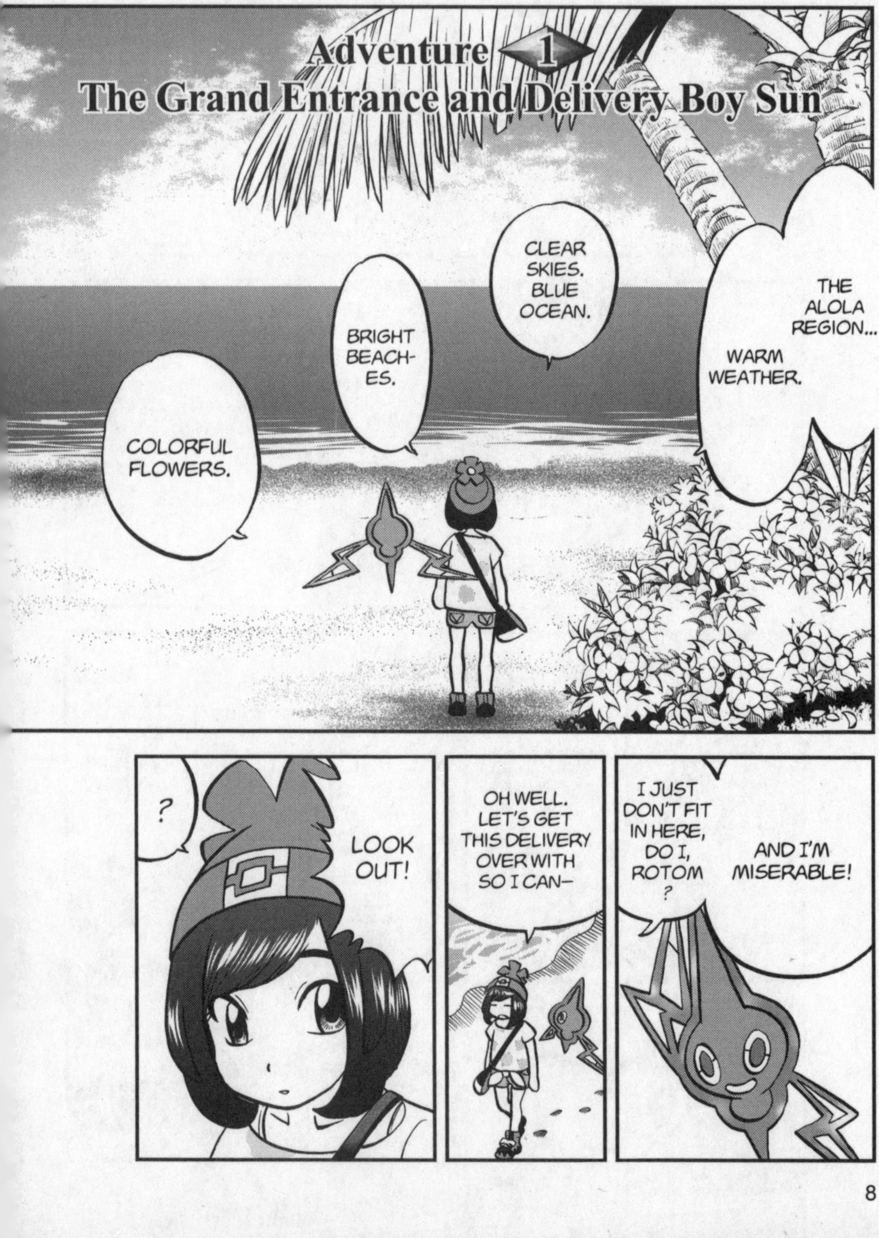

THE ALOLA REGION...
WARM WEATHER.
CLEAR SKIES. BLUE OCEAN.
BRIGHT BEACH-ES.
COLORFUL FLOWERS.
I JUST DON'T FIT IN HERE, DO I, ROTOM?
AND I'M MISERABLE!
OH WELL. LET'S GET THIS DELIVERY OVER WITH SO I CAN—
LOOK OUT!
?

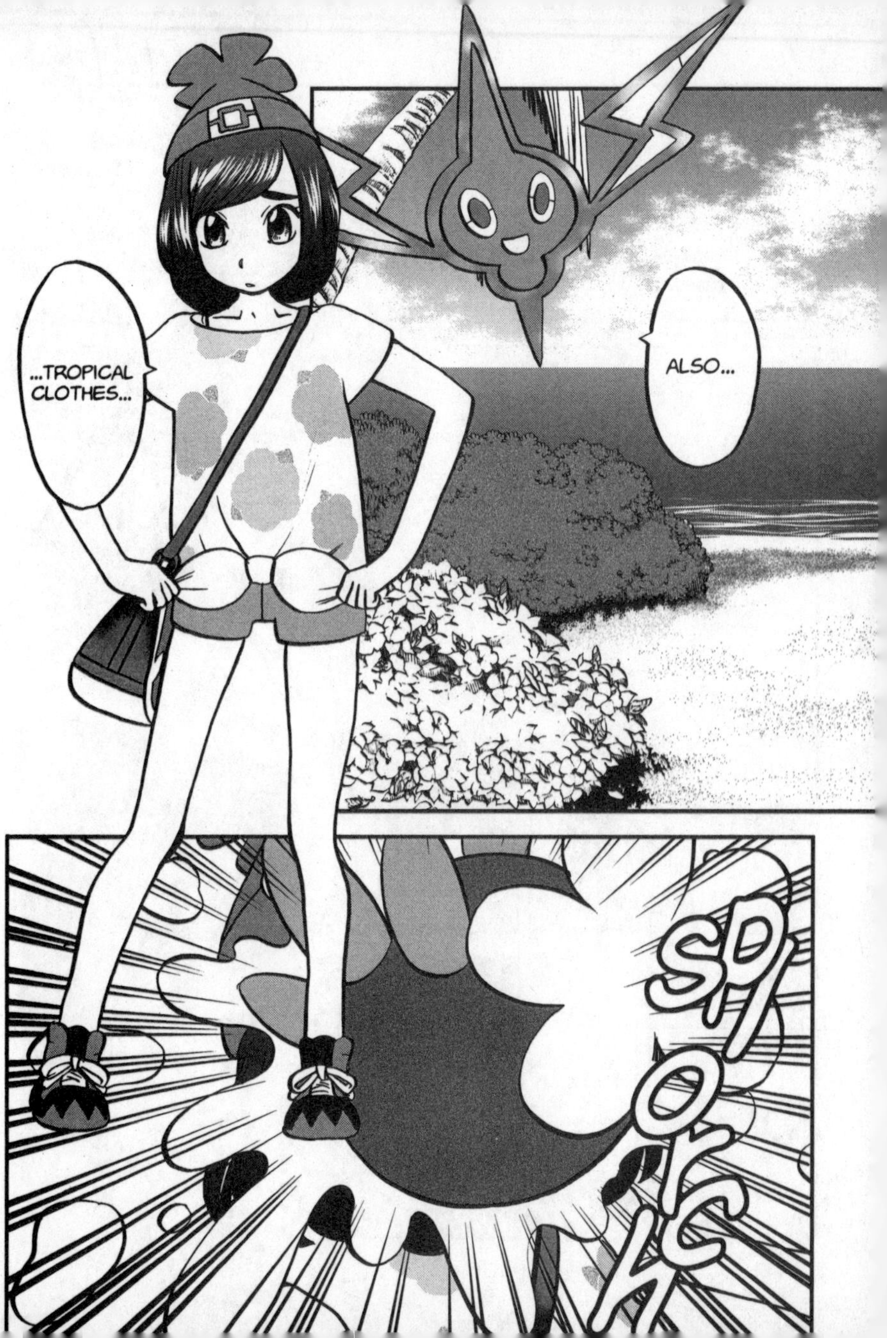
ALSO...
...TROPICAL CLOTHES...
SPLOTCH

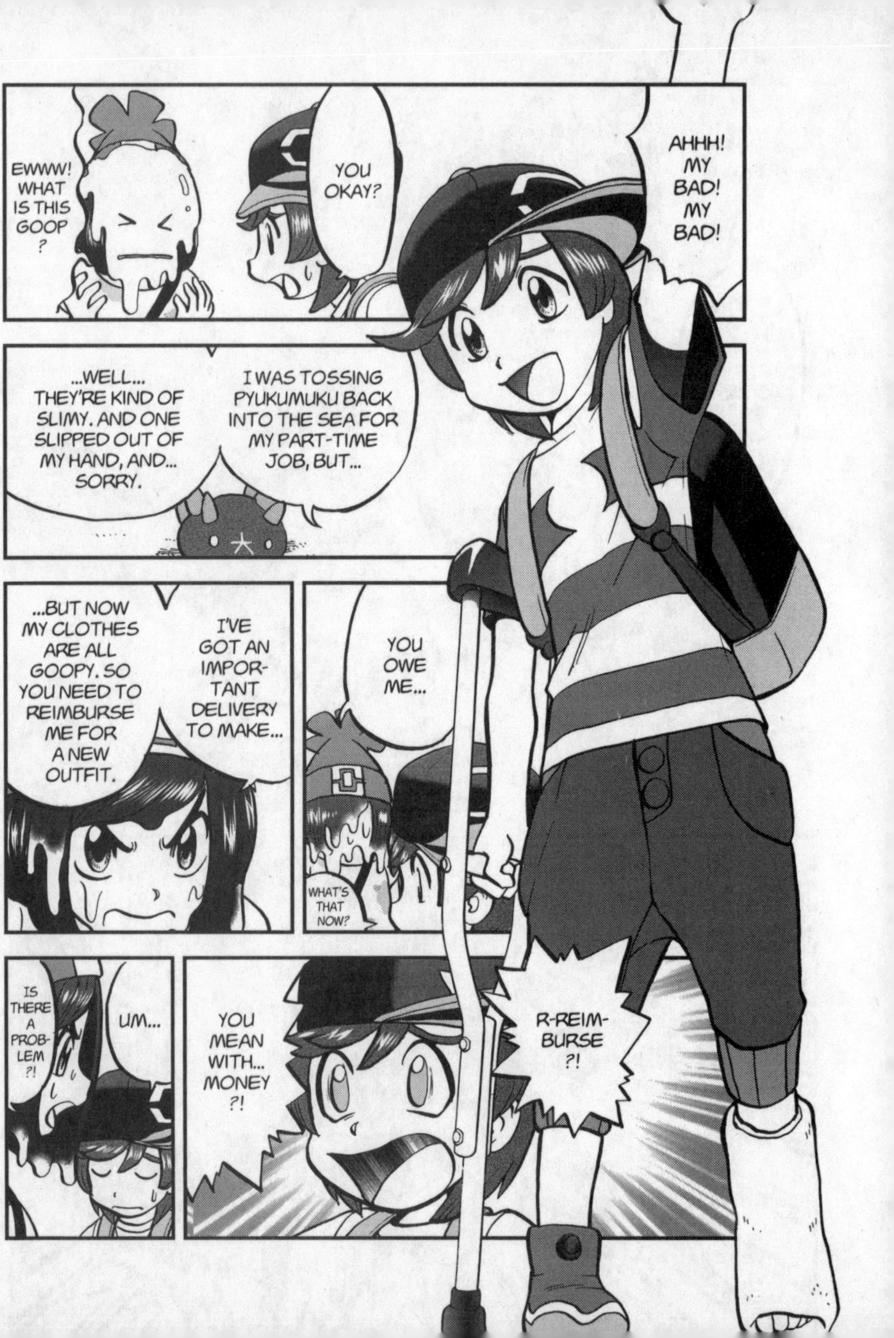
AHHH! MY BAD! MY BAD!
YOU OKAY?
EWWW! WHAT IS THIS GOOP?
I WAS TOSSING PYUKUMUKU BACK INTO THE SEA FOR MY PART-TIME JOB, BUT...
...WELL... THEY'RE KIND OF SLIMY. AND ONE SLIPPED OUT OF MY HAND, AND... SORRY.
YOU OWE ME...
WHAT'S THAT NOW?
I'VE GOT AN IMPOR-TANT DELIVERY TO MAKE...
...BUT NOW MY CLOTHES ARE ALL GOOPY. SO YOU NEED TO REIMBURSE ME FOR A NEW OUTFIT.
R-REIM-BURSE?!
YOU MEAN WITH... MONEY?!
UM...
IS THERE A PROB-LEM?!

...NOT
!

!bodoink

YOU'RE RIGHT! MY SKIN FEELS SO SILKY SMOOTH NOW! I CAN'T THANK YOU ENOUGH...

ALL THE CELEBRITIES ARE USING IT. SO, ACTUALLY, YOU OUGHT TO BE GRATE—

...THAT PYUKUMUKU GOOP IS AN EXCELLENT MOISTUR- IZER!

BUT
...

WHAT KIND OF A PART- TIME JOB IS THAT ANY- WAY?!

SPLASH

NO, NO! YOU'RE SUPPOSED TO THROW THE PYUKUMUKU BACK INTO THE SEA! AS FAR AS YOU CAN, TOO!

SEE
...?

rstl rstl

PYUKU- MUKU, THE SEA CUCUM- BER POKÉ- MON...

I THINK THEY'RE CUTE, BUT THE TOURISTS FREAK OUT WHEN THEY SEE A LOT OF THEM LYING ALL OVER THE BEACH.

№ 200 Pyukumuku

JPN | ENG | FRA | GER | ITA | KOR | SPA | CHS | CHT

Water

Sea Cucumber Pokémon

Height: 1'00" Weight: 2.6 lbs.

These Pokémon line the beaches. The sticky mucus that covers their bodies can be used to soothe sunburned skin. How convenient!

Appearance/Cry   Habitat

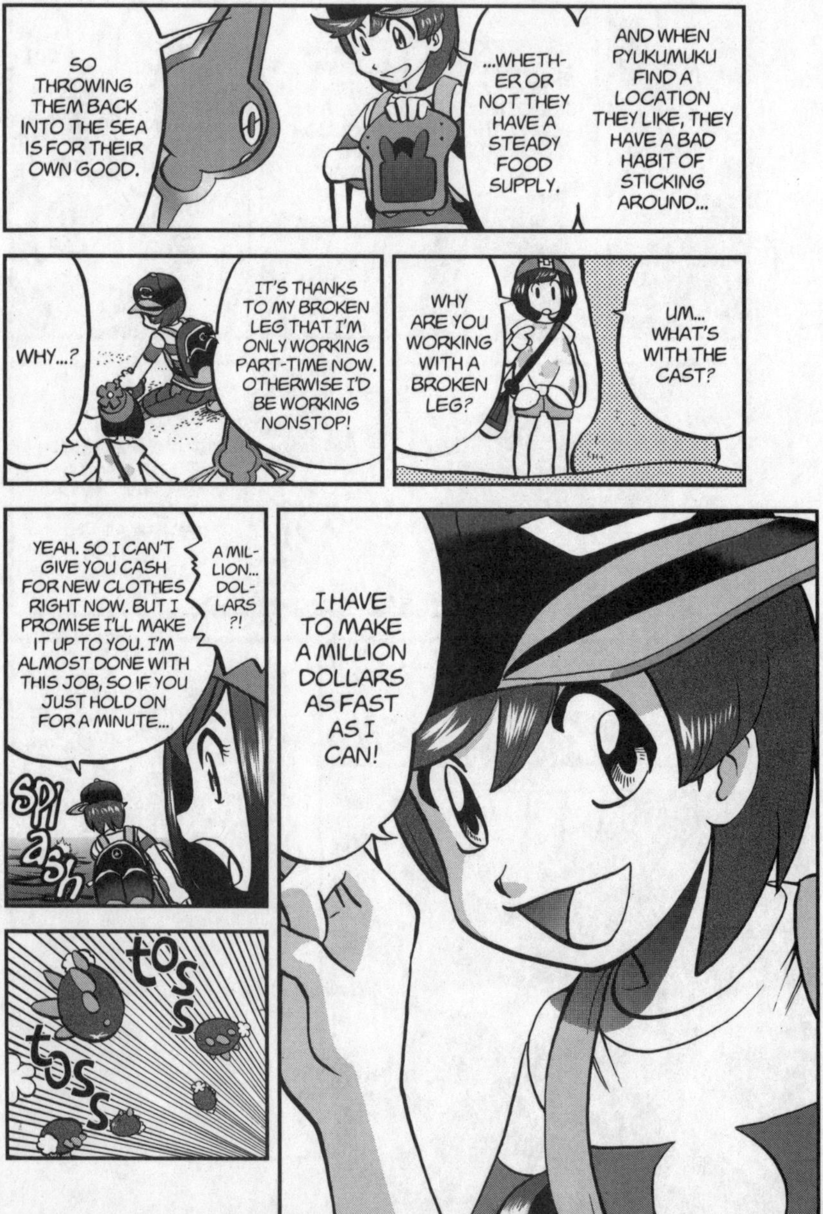
AND WHEN PYUKUMUKU FIND A LOCATION THEY LIKE, THEY HAVE A BAD HABIT OF STICKING AROUND...
...WHETHER OR NOT THEY HAVE A STEADY FOOD SUPPLY.
SO THROWING THEM BACK INTO THE SEA IS FOR THEIR OWN GOOD.
UM... WHAT'S WITH THE CAST?
WHY ARE YOU WORKING WITH A BROKEN LEG?
IT'S THANKS TO MY BROKEN LEG THAT I'M ONLY WORKING PART-TIME NOW. OTHERWISE I'D BE WORKING NONSTOP!
WHY...?
I HAVE TO MAKE A MILLION DOLLARS AS FAST AS I CAN!
A MILLION... DOLLARS?!
YEAH. SO I CAN'T GIVE YOU CASH FOR NEW CLOTHES RIGHT NOW. BUT I PROMISE I'LL MAKE IT UP TO YOU. I'M ALMOST DONE WITH THIS JOB, SO IF YOU JUST HOLD ON FOR A MINUTE...
SPLASH
TOSS
TOSS

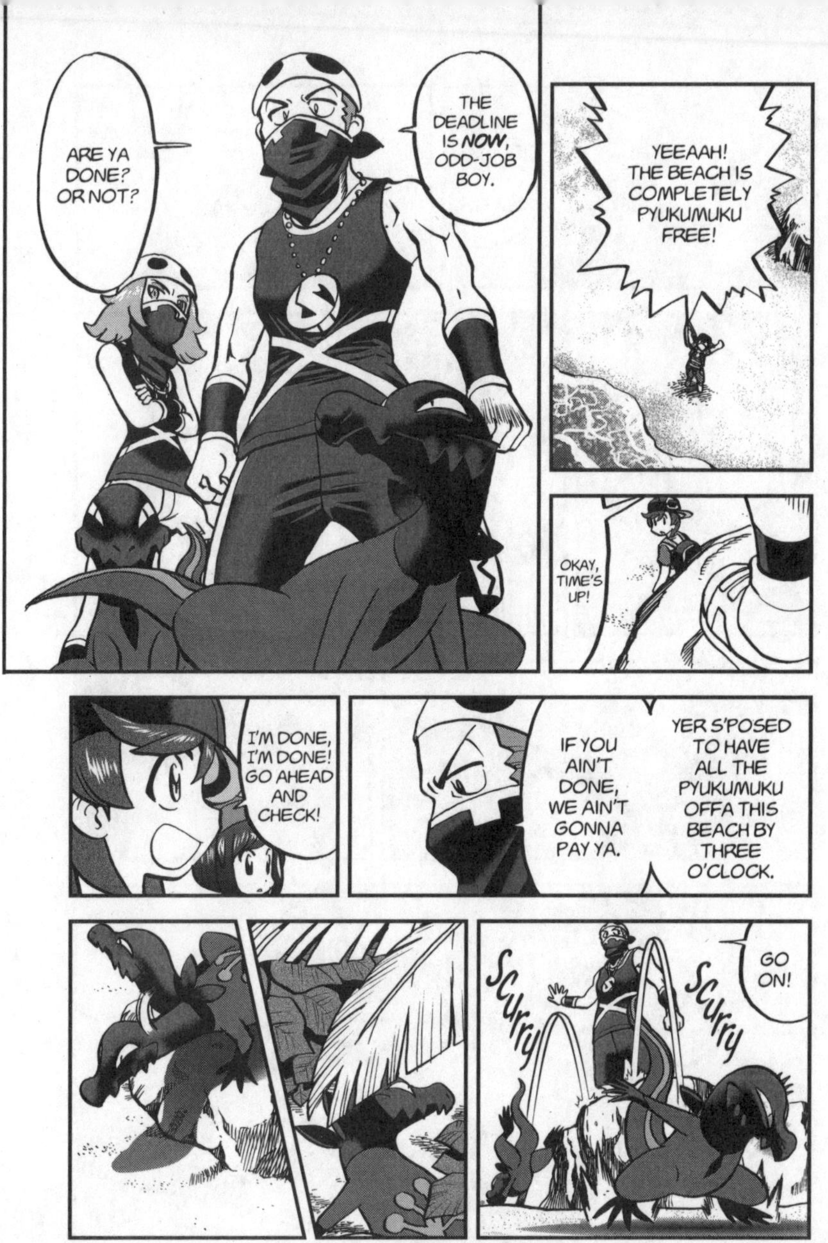
YEEAAH! THE BEACH IS COMPLETELY PYUKUMUKU FREE!
OKAY, TIME'S UP!
THE DEADLINE IS **NOW**, ODD-JOB BOY.
ARE YA DONE? OR NOT?
YER S'POSED TO HAVE ALL THE PYUKUMUKU OFFA THIS BEACH BY THREE O'CLOCK.
IF YOU AIN'T DONE, WE AIN'T GONNA PAY YA.
I'M DONE, I'M DONE! GO AHEAD AND CHECK!
GO ON!
SCURRY
SCURRY

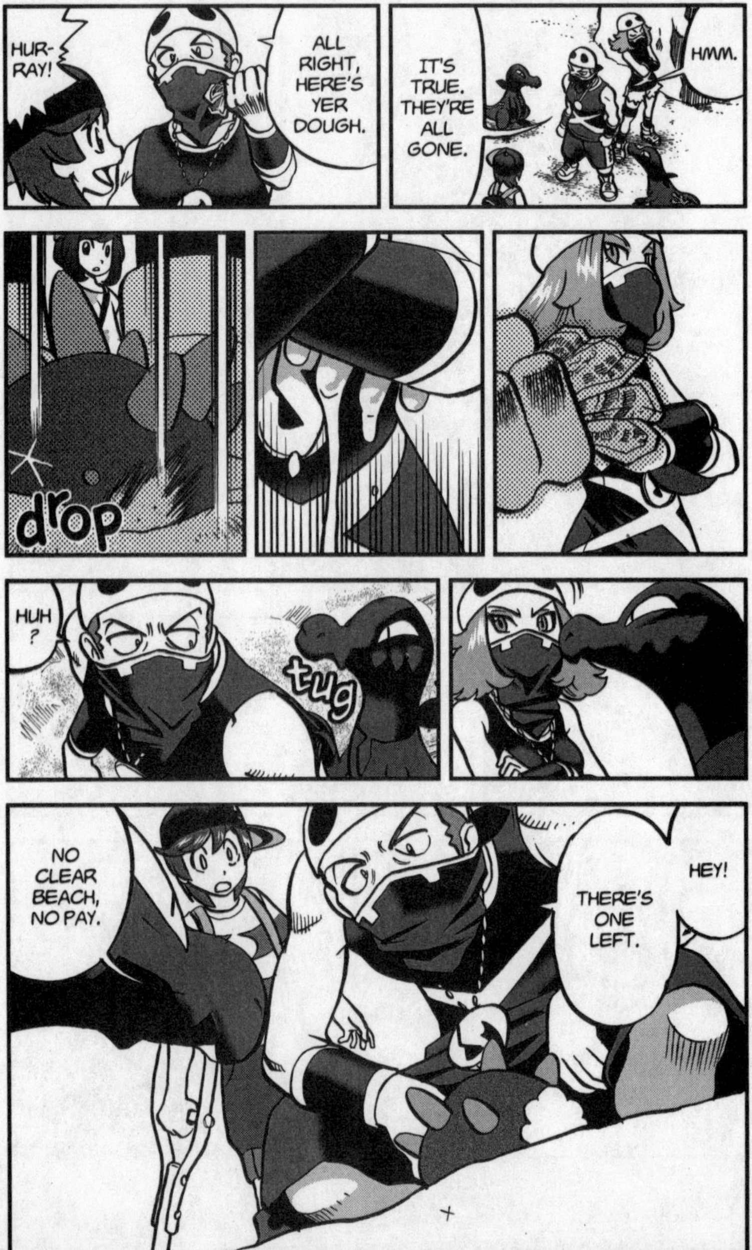
HMM.
IT'S TRUE. THEY'RE ALL GONE.
ALL RIGHT, HERE'S YER DOUGH.
HUR-RAY!
drop
HUH?
tug
HEY!
THERE'S ONE LEFT.
NO CLEAR BEACH, NO PAY.

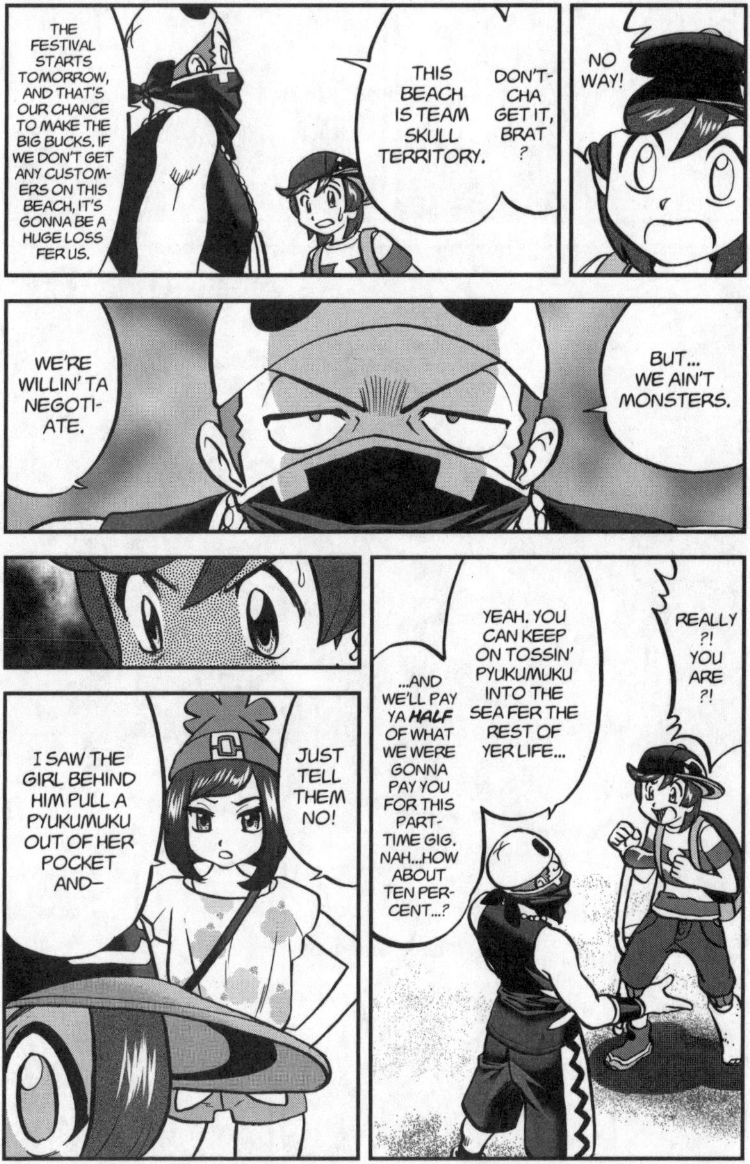
NO WAY!
DON'T-CHA GET IT, BRAT?
THIS BEACH IS TEAM SKULL TERRITORY.
THE FESTIVAL STARTS TOMORROW, AND THAT'S OUR CHANCE TO MAKE THE BIG BUCKS. IF WE DON'T GET ANY CUSTOMERS ON THIS BEACH, IT'S GONNA BE A HUGE LOSS FER US.
BUT... WE AIN'T MONSTERS.
WE'RE WILLIN' TA NEGOTIATE.
REALLY?! YOU ARE?!
YEAH. YOU CAN KEEP ON TOSSIN' PYUKUMUKU INTO THE SEA FER THE REST OF YER LIFE...
...AND WE'LL PAY YA HALF OF WHAT WE WERE GONNA PAY YOU FOR THIS PART-TIME GIG. NAH...HOW ABOUT TEN PERCENT...?
JUST TELL THEM NO!
I SAW THE GIRL BEHIND HIM PULL A PYUKUMUKU OUT OF HER POCKET AND—

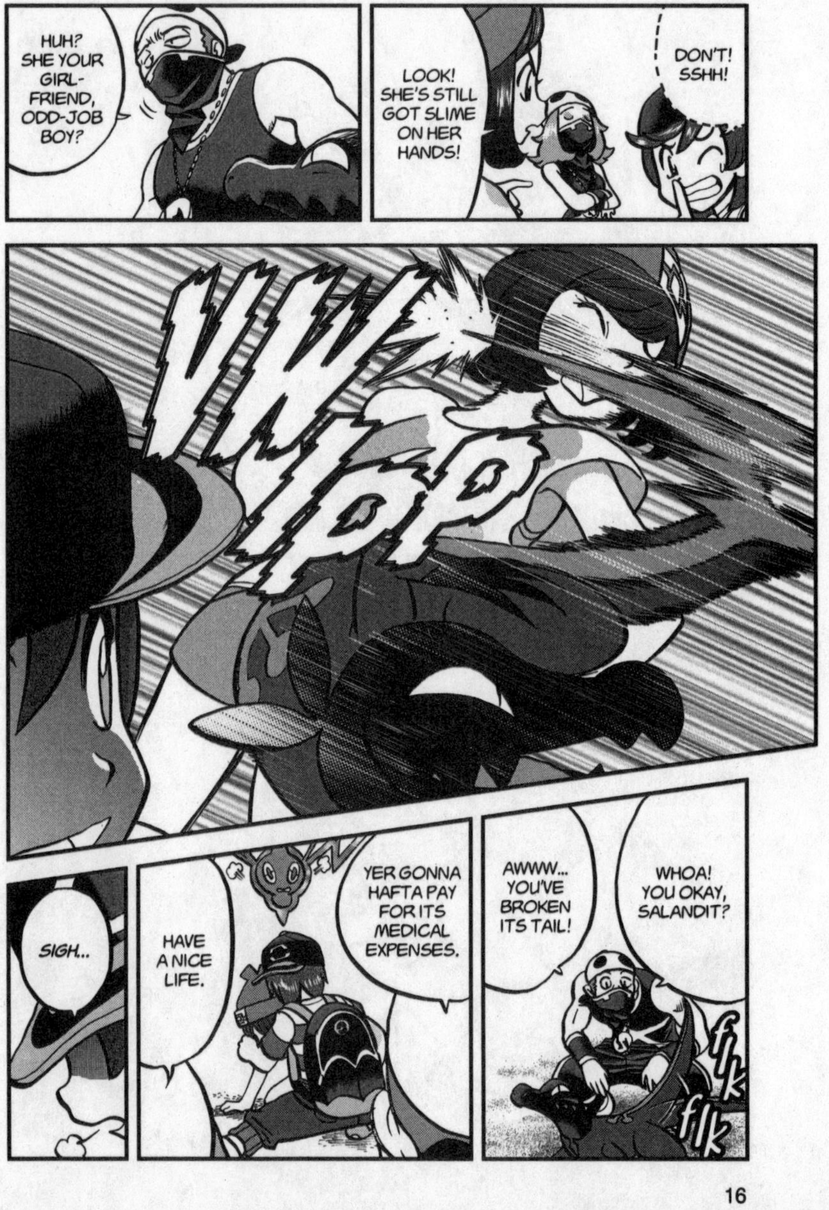
DON'T! SSHH!
LOOK! SHE'S STILL GOT SLIME ON HER HANDS!
HUH? SHE YOUR GIRL-FRIEND, ODD-JOB BOY?
VWIPP
WHOA! YOU OKAY, SALANDIT?
AWWW... YOU'VE BROKEN ITS TAIL!
flk flk
YER GONNA HAFTA PAY FOR ITS MEDICAL EXPENSES.
HAVE A NICE LIFE.
SIGH...

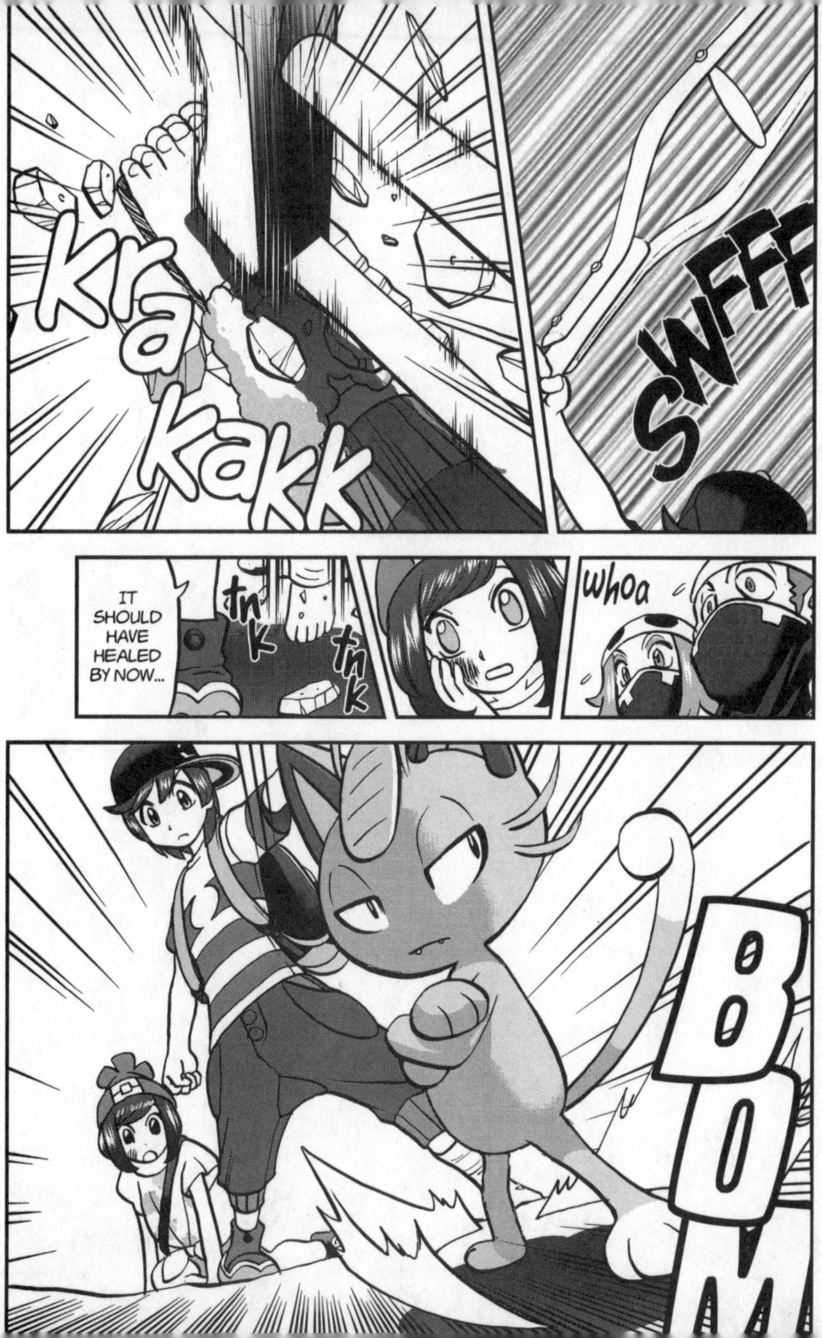
SWFFF
krakakk
whoa
IT SHOULD HAVE HEALED BY NOW...
tnk
tnk
BOOM

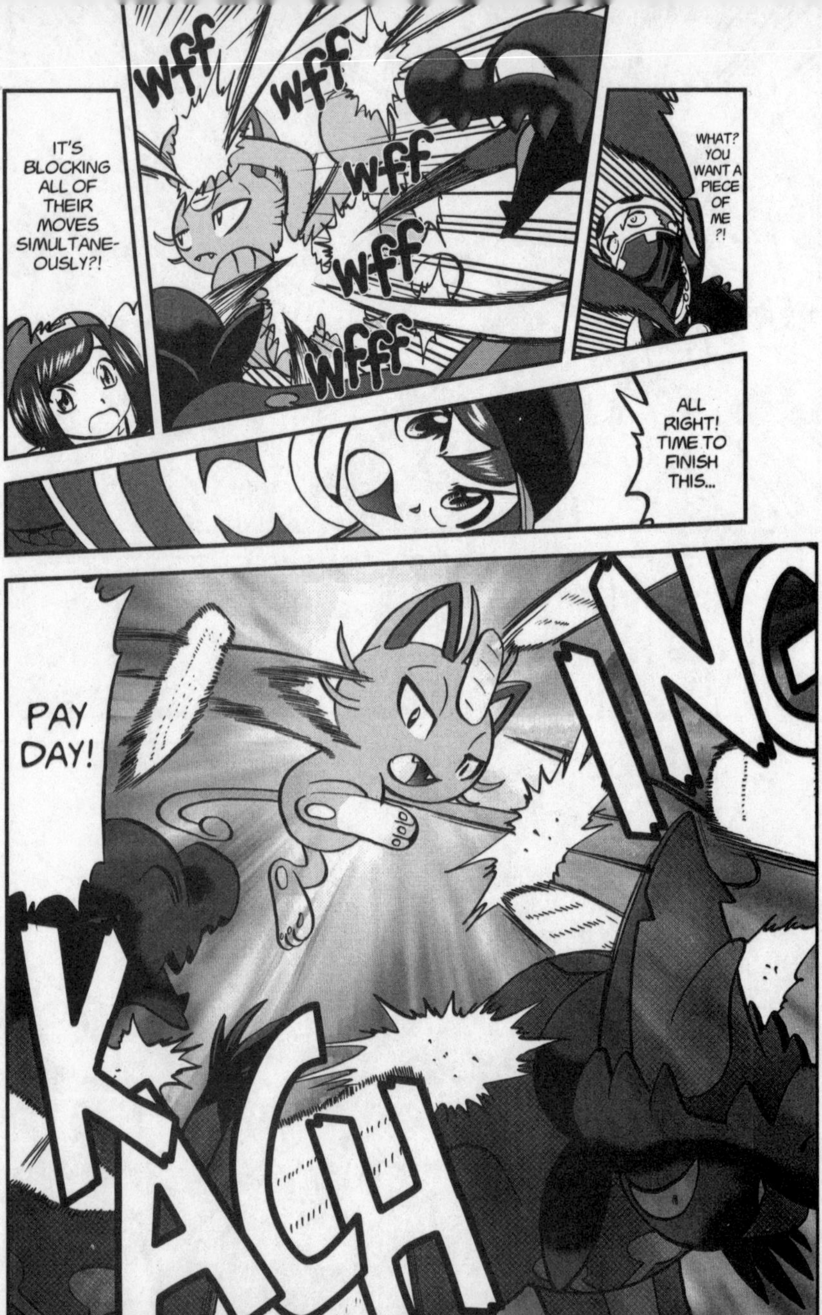
WHAT? YOU WANT A PIECE OF ME?!
wff
wff
wff
wff
wff
wff
IT'S BLOCKING ALL OF THEIR MOVES SIMULTANE-OUSLY?!
ALL RIGHT! TIME TO FINISH THIS...
PAY DAY!
KACH
ING

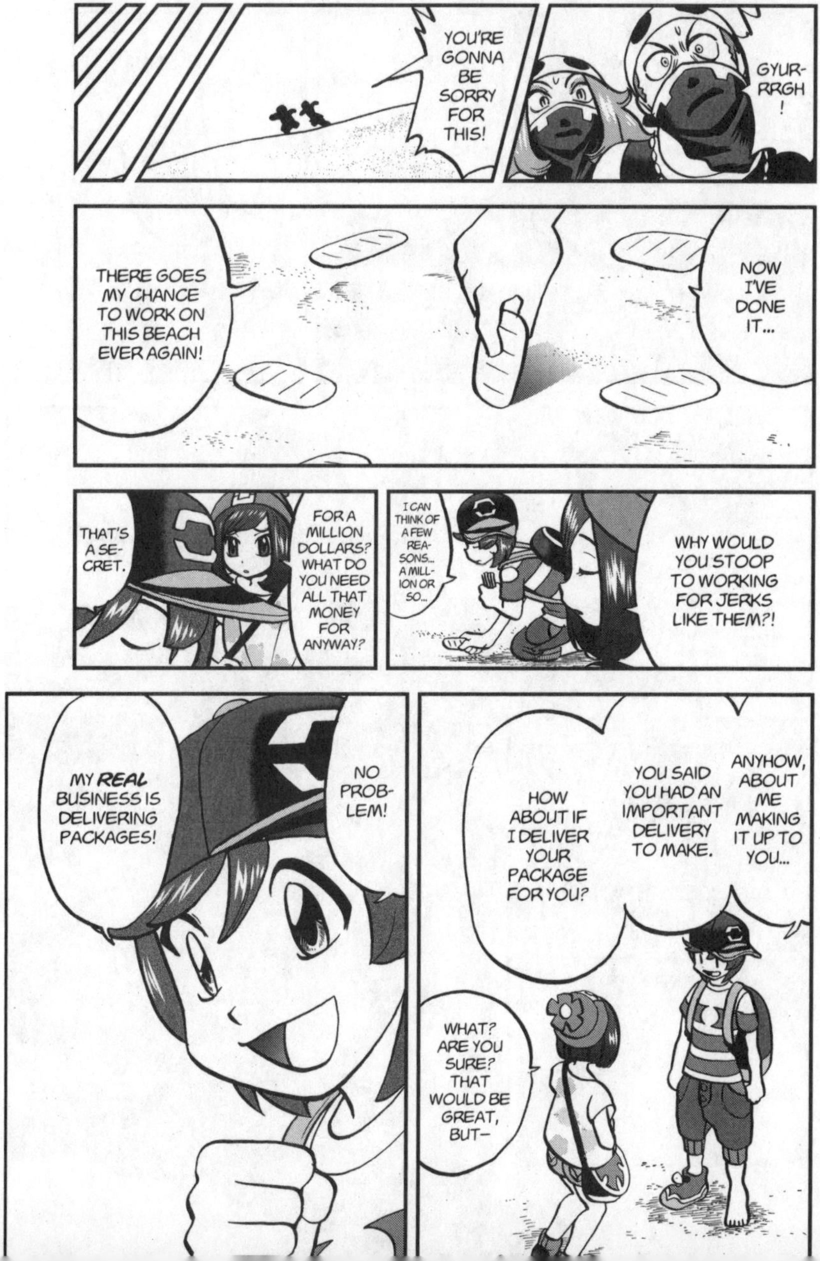
GYURRRGH!
YOU'RE GONNA BE SORRY FOR THIS!
NOW I'VE DONE IT...
THERE GOES MY CHANCE TO WORK ON THIS BEACH EVER AGAIN!
WHY WOULD YOU STOOP TO WORKING FOR JERKS LIKE THEM?!
I CAN THINK OF A FEW REASONS... A MILLION OR SO...
FOR A MILLION DOLLARS? WHAT DO YOU NEED ALL THAT MONEY FOR ANYWAY?
THAT'S A SECRET.
ANYHOW, ABOUT ME MAKING IT UP TO YOU...
YOU SAID YOU HAD AN IMPORTANT DELIVERY TO MAKE.
HOW ABOUT IF I DELIVER YOUR PACKAGE FOR YOU?
WHAT? ARE YOU SURE? THAT WOULD BE GREAT, BUT–
NO PROBLEM!
MY *REAL* BUSINESS IS DELIVERING PACKAGES!

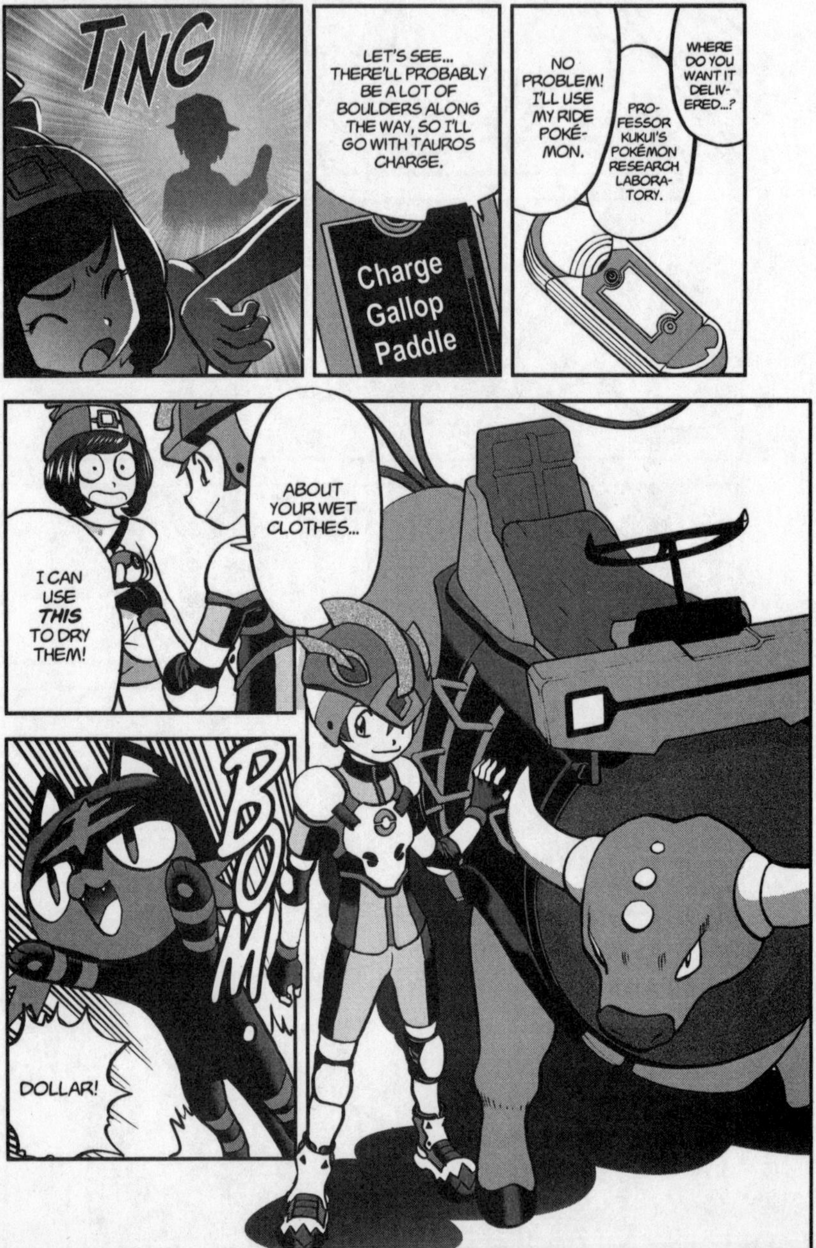
WHERE DO YOU WANT IT DELIVERED...?
PROFESSOR KUKUI'S POKÉMON RESEARCH LABORATORY.
NO PROBLEM! I'LL USE MY RIDE POKÉMON.
LET'S SEE... THERE'LL PROBABLY BE A LOT OF BOULDERS ALONG THE WAY, SO I'LL GO WITH TAUROS CHARGE.
Charge
Gallop
Paddle
TING
ABOUT YOUR WET CLOTHES...
I CAN USE THIS TO DRY THEM!
BOOM
DOLLAR!

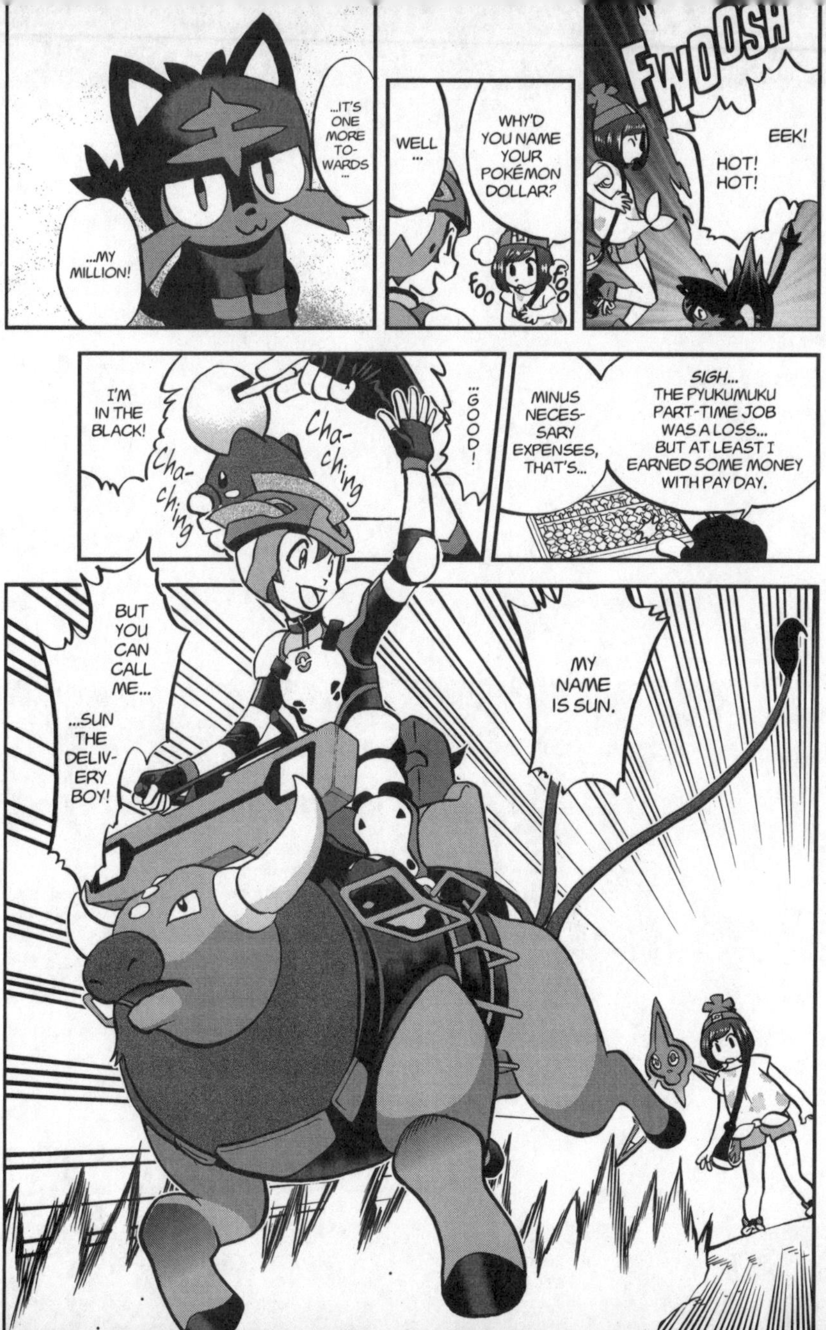
FWOOSH
EEK!
HOT! HOT!
WHY'D YOU NAME YOUR POKÉMON DOLLAR?
WELL ...
FOO
FOO
...IT'S ONE MORE TO-WARDS ...
...MY MILLION!
SIGH... THE PYUKUMUKU PART-TIME JOB WAS A LOSS... BUT AT LEAST I EARNED SOME MONEY WITH PAY DAY.
MINUS NECES-SARY EXPENSES, THAT'S...
...GOOD!
I'M IN THE BLACK!
Cha-ching
Cha-ching
Cha-ching
MY NAME IS SUN.
BUT YOU CAN CALL ME...
...SUN THE DELIV-ERY BOY!

🌺 A Cheerful Greeting

Here in the Alola region, people greet each other with the word "Alola."

♪

It can mean hello, goodbye and so on, and can be used in a variety of situations. It's even more expressive when you say it while moving both hands in front of your chest in a circle.

♪

Guide to Alola 1

Adventure 2
The Delivery of Rotom and the Girl

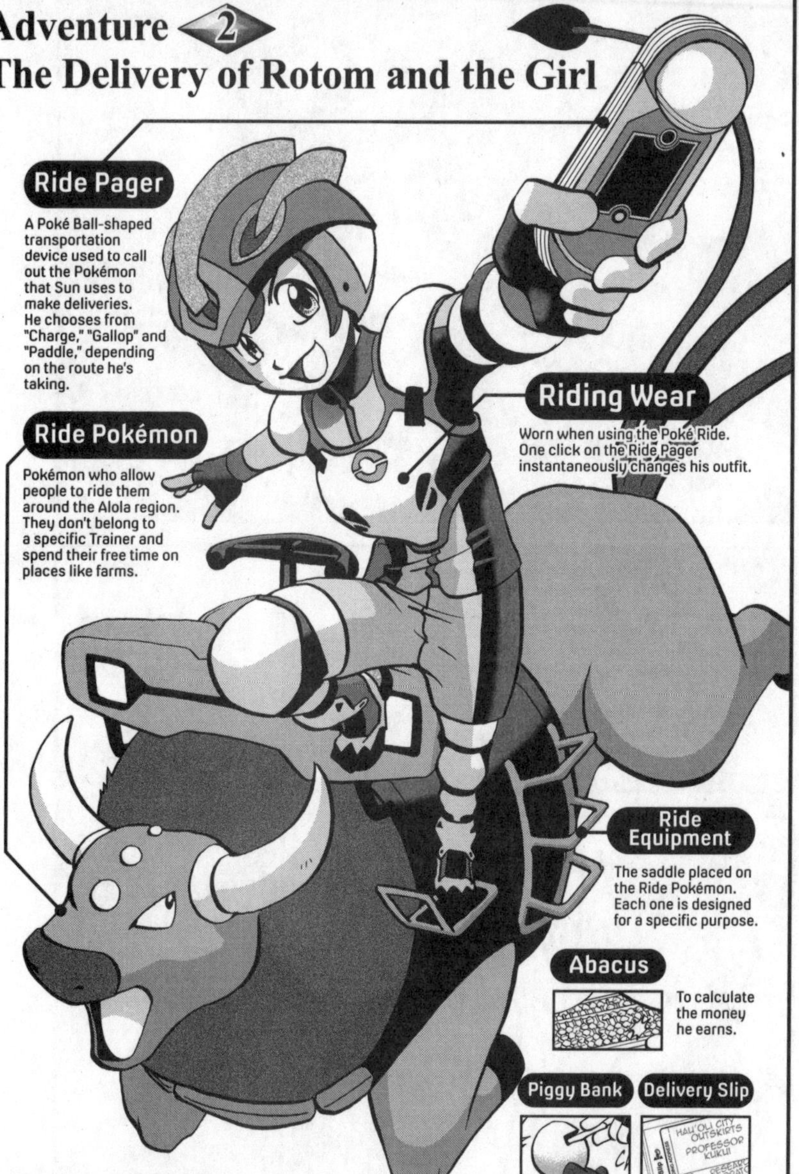

Ride Pager
A Poké Ball-shaped transportation device used to call out the Pokémon that Sun uses to make deliveries. He chooses from "Charge," "Gallop" and "Paddle," depending on the route he's taking.
Ride Pokémon
Pokémon who allow people to ride them around the Alola region. They don't belong to a specific Trainer and spend their free time on places like farms.
Riding Wear
Worn when using the Poké Ride. One click on the Ride Pager instantaneously changes his outfit.
Ride Equipment
The saddle placed on the Ride Pokémon. Each one is designed for a specific purpose.
Abacus
To calculate the money he earns.
Piggy Bank
To save a little of everything he earns.
Delivery Slip
HAU'OLI CITY OUTSKIRTS
PROFESSOR KUKUI
To record a customer's information.

Check out the secrets of Sun's delivery service!

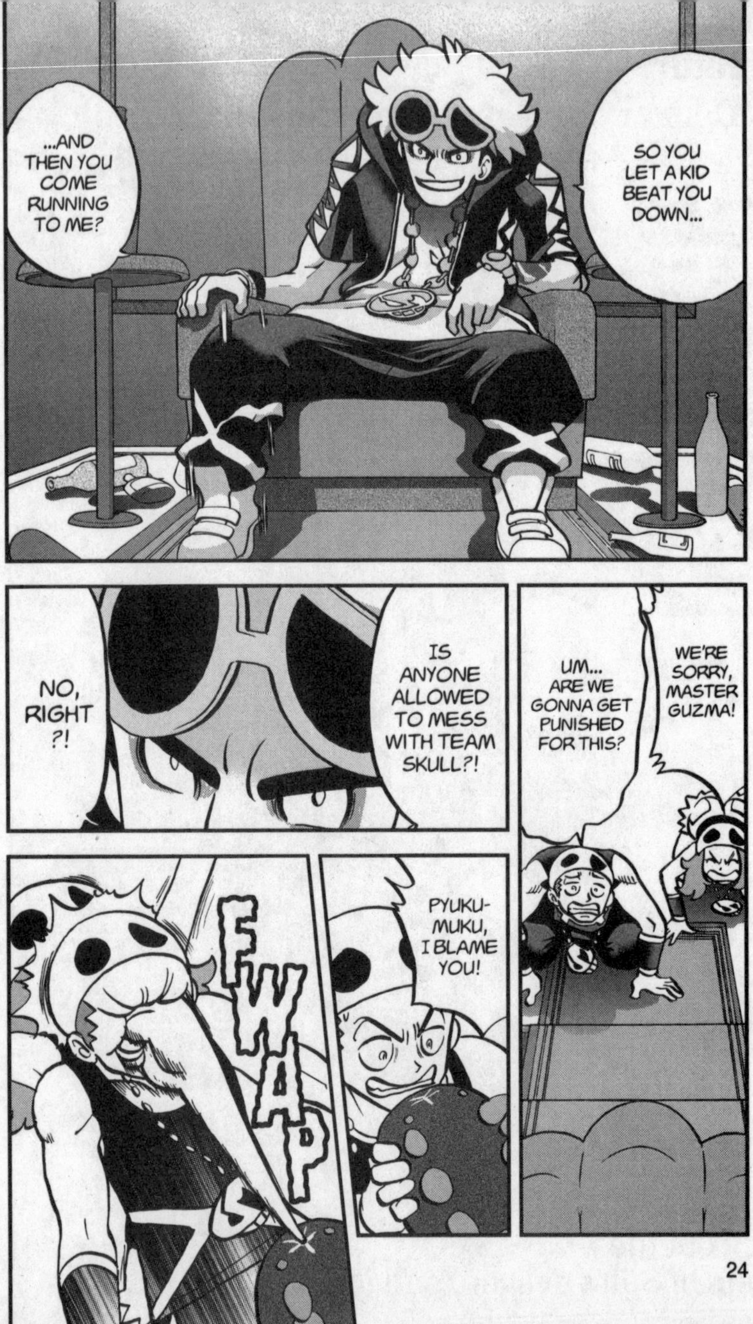
SO YOU LET A KID BEAT YOU DOWN...
...AND THEN YOU COME RUNNING TO ME?
WE'RE SORRY, MASTER GUZMA!
UM... ARE WE GONNA GET PUNISHED FOR THIS?
IS ANYONE ALLOWED TO MESS WITH TEAM SKULL?!
NO, RIGHT ?!
PYUKU-MUKU, I BLAME YOU!
FWAP

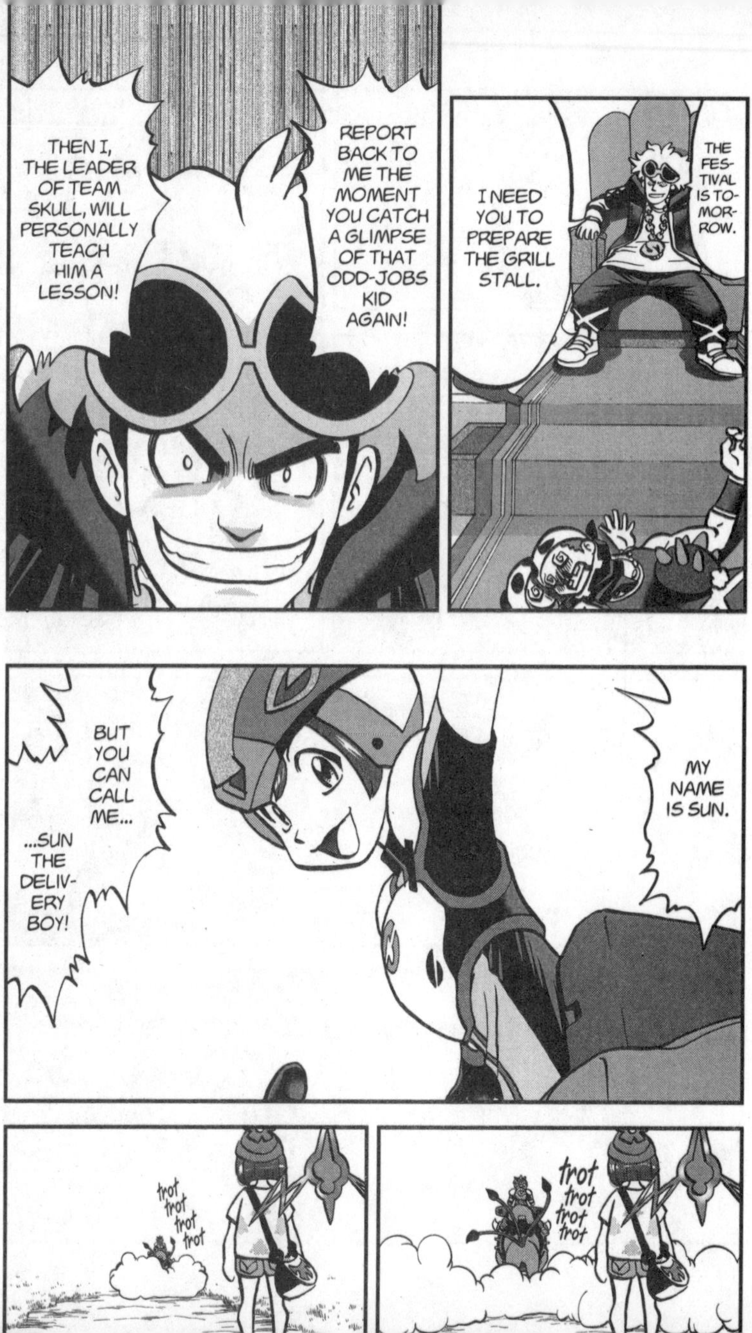
THE FES-TIVAL IS TO-MOR-ROW.
I NEED YOU TO PREPARE THE GRILL STALL.
REPORT BACK TO ME THE MOMENT YOU CATCH A GLIMPSE OF THAT ODD-JOBS KID AGAIN!
THEN I, THE LEADER OF TEAM SKULL, WILL PERSONALLY TEACH HIM A LESSON!
MY NAME IS SUN.
BUT YOU CAN CALL ME...
...SUN THE DELIV-ERY BOY!
trot trot trot trot trot
trot trot trot trot

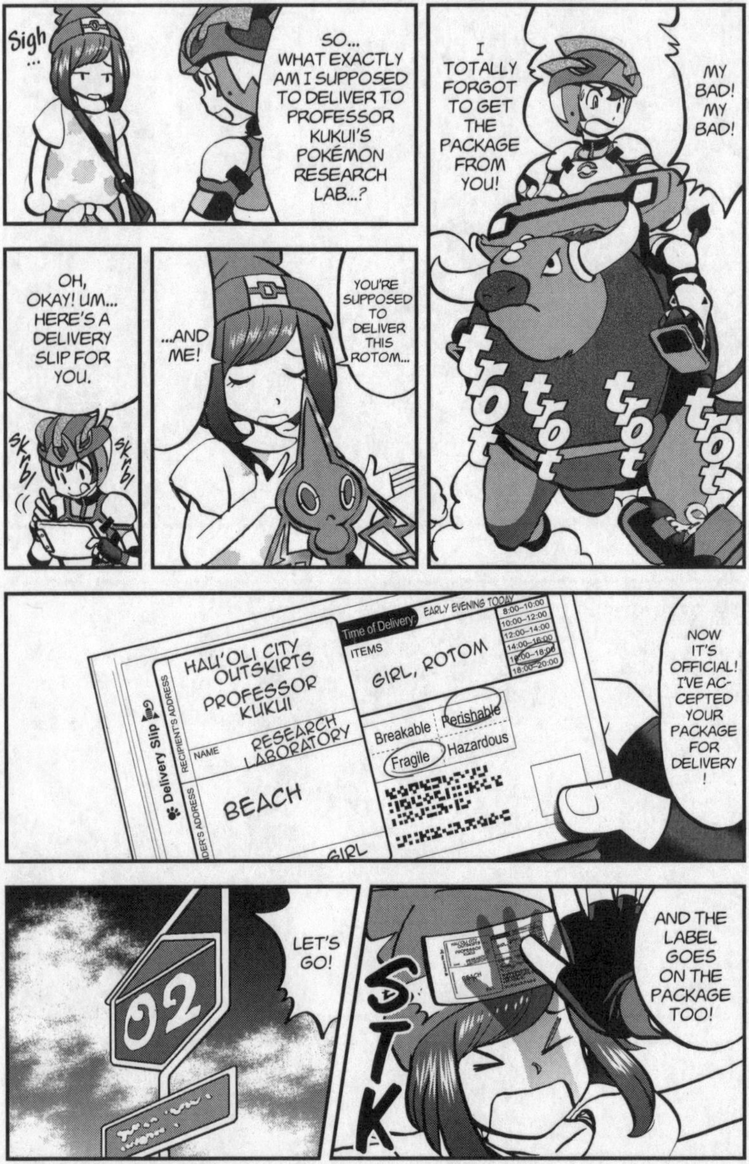
MY BAD! MY BAD!
I TOTALLY FORGOT TO GET THE PACKAGE FROM YOU!
trot trot trot trot
SO... WHAT EXACTLY AM I SUPPOSED TO DELIVER TO PROFESSOR KUKUI'S POKÉMON RESEARCH LAB...?
Sigh...
YOU'RE SUPPOSED TO DELIVER THIS ROTOM...
...AND ME!
OH, OKAY! UM... HERE'S A DELIVERY SLIP FOR YOU.
SKRBL SKRBL
NOW IT'S OFFICIAL! I'VE ACCEPTED YOUR PACKAGE FOR DELIVERY!
Time of Delivery: EARLY EVENING TODAY
8:00–10:00
10:00–12:00
12:00–14:00
14:00–16:00
16:00–18:00
18:00–20:00
ITEMS
GIRL, ROTOM
Delivery Slip
RECIPIENT'S ADDRESS
HAU'OLI CITY OUTSKIRTS PROFESSOR KUKUI
NAME
RESEARCH LABORATORY
Breakable
Perishable
Fragile
Hazardous
SENDER'S ADDRESS
BEACH
GIRL
AND THE LABEL GOES ON THE PACKAGE TOO!
STK
LET'S GO!
02

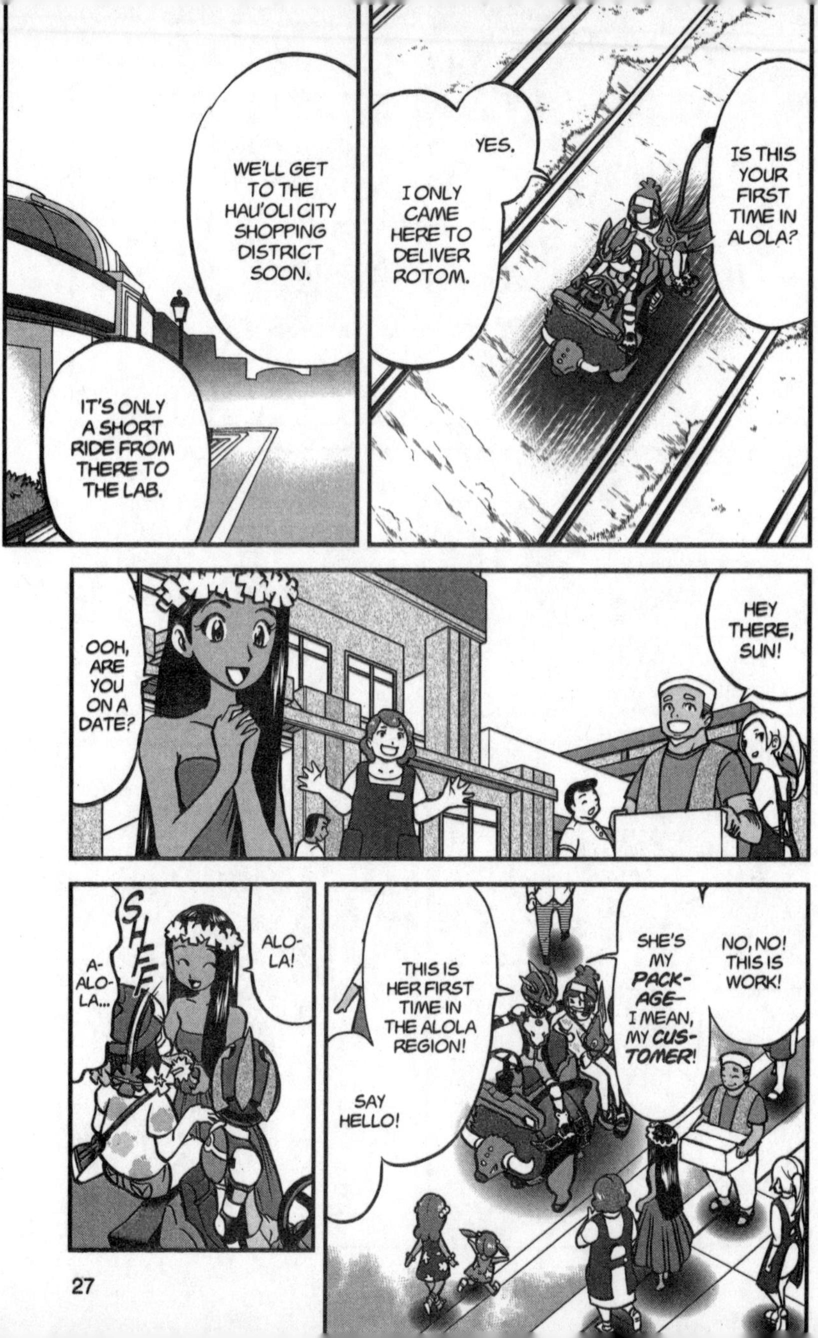
IS THIS YOUR FIRST TIME IN ALOLA?
YES.
I ONLY CAME HERE TO DELIVER ROTOM.
WE'LL GET TO THE HAU'OLI CITY SHOPPING DISTRICT SOON.
IT'S ONLY A SHORT RIDE FROM THERE TO THE LAB.
HEY THERE, SUN!
OOH, ARE YOU ON A DATE?
NO, NO! THIS IS WORK!
SHE'S MY PACKAGE— I MEAN, MY CUSTOMER!
THIS IS HER FIRST TIME IN THE ALOLA REGION!
SAY HELLO!
ALO-LA!
SHFF
A-ALO-LA...

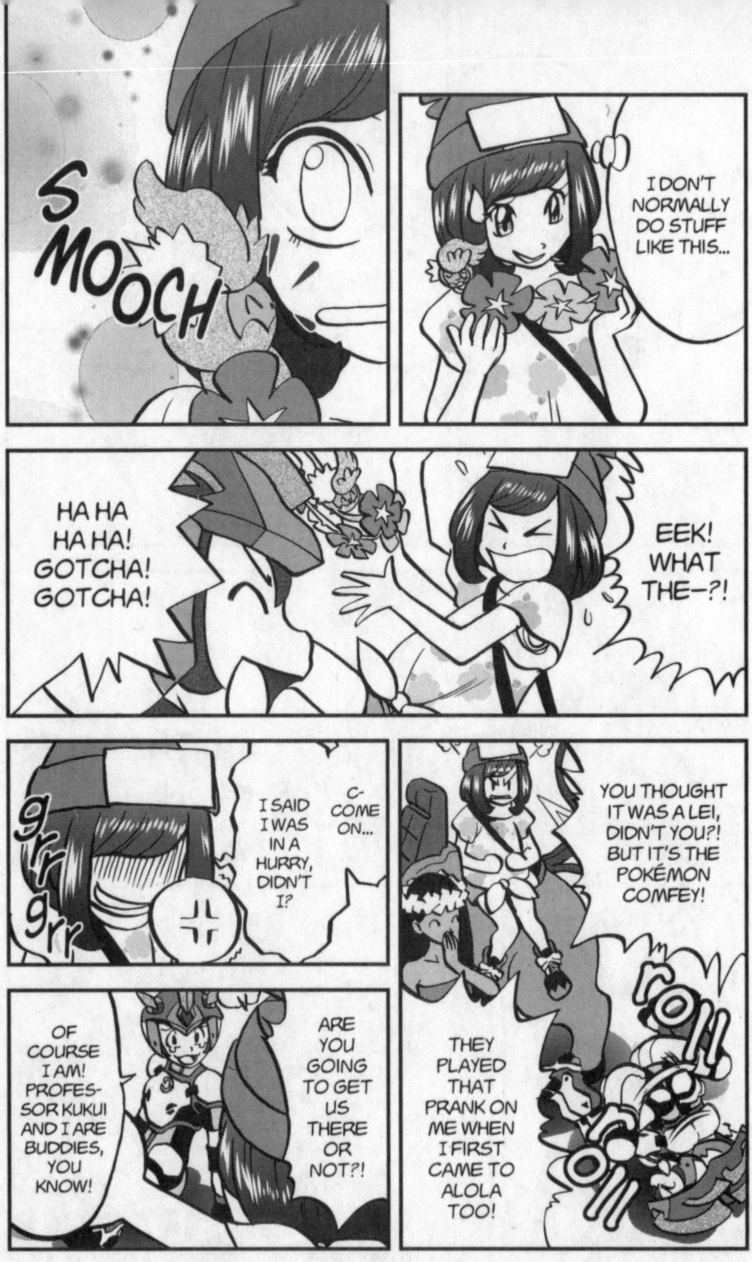
I DON'T NORMALLY DO STUFF LIKE THIS...
SMOOCH
EEK! WHAT THE–?!
HA HA HA HA! GOTCHA! GOTCHA!
YOU THOUGHT IT WAS A LEI, DIDN'T YOU?! BUT IT'S THE POKÉMON COMFEY!
THEY PLAYED THAT PRANK ON ME WHEN I FIRST CAME TO ALOLA TOO!
roll roll
C-COME ON...
I SAID I WAS IN A HURRY, DIDN'T I?
grr grr
ARE YOU GOING TO GET US THERE OR NOT?!
OF COURSE I AM! PROFES-SOR KUKUI AND I ARE BUDDIES, YOU KNOW!

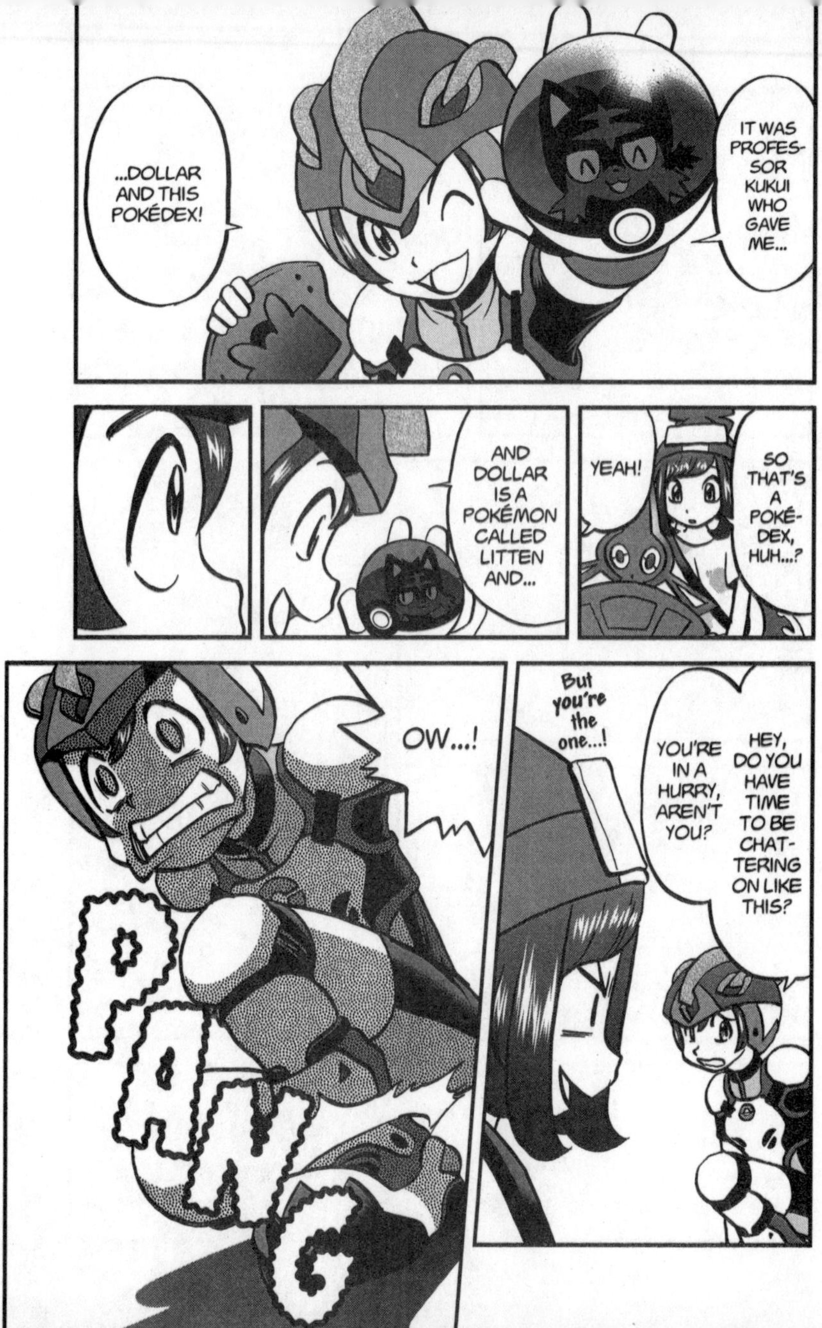
IT WAS PROFES-SOR KUKUI WHO GAVE ME...
...DOLLAR AND THIS POKÉDEX!
SO THAT'S A POKÉ-DEX, HUH...?
YEAH!
AND DOLLAR IS A POKÉMON CALLED LITTEN AND...
HEY, DO YOU HAVE TIME TO BE CHAT-TERING ON LIKE THIS?
YOU'RE IN A HURRY, AREN'T YOU?
But you're the one...!
OW...!
PANG

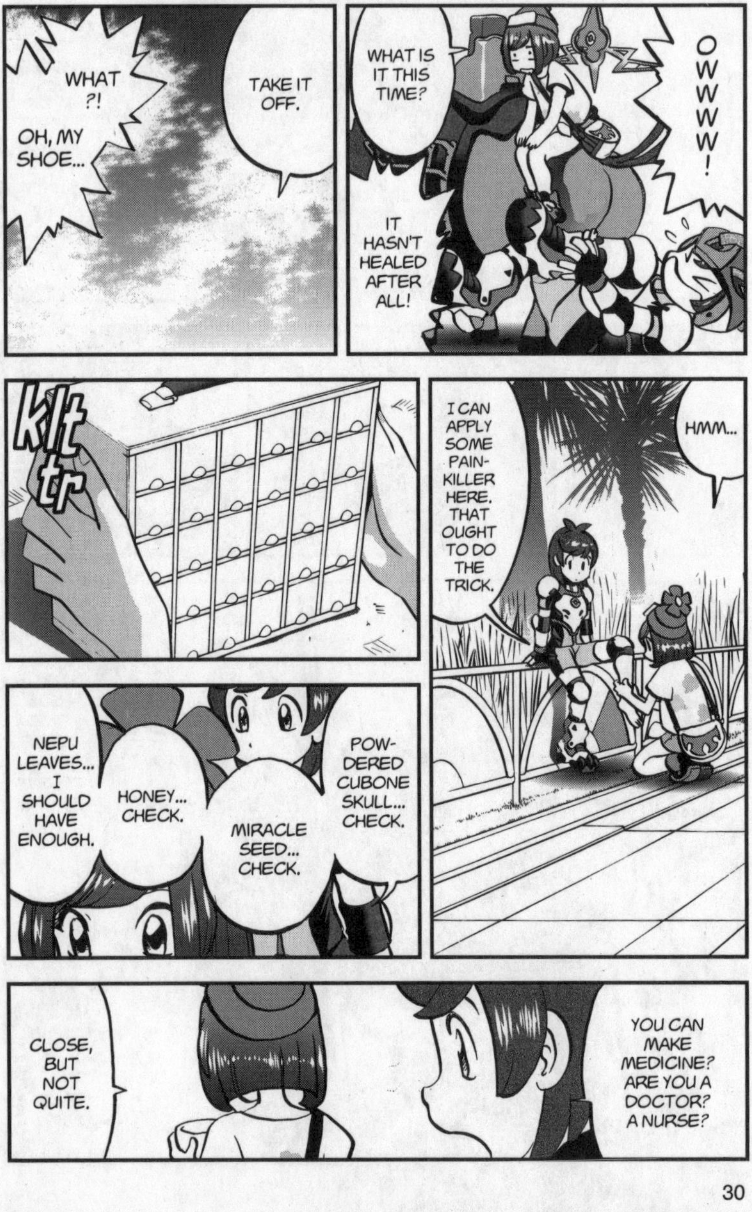
OWWWWW!
WHAT IS IT THIS TIME?
IT HASN'T HEALED AFTER ALL!
TAKE IT OFF.
WHAT?!
OH, MY SHOE...
HMM...
I CAN APPLY SOME PAIN-KILLER HERE. THAT OUGHT TO DO THE TRICK.
klt tr
POW-DERED CUBONE SKULL... CHECK.
MIRACLE SEED... CHECK.
HONEY... CHECK.
NEPU LEAVES... I SHOULD HAVE ENOUGH.
YOU CAN MAKE MEDICINE? ARE YOU A DOCTOR? A NURSE?
CLOSE, BUT NOT QUITE.

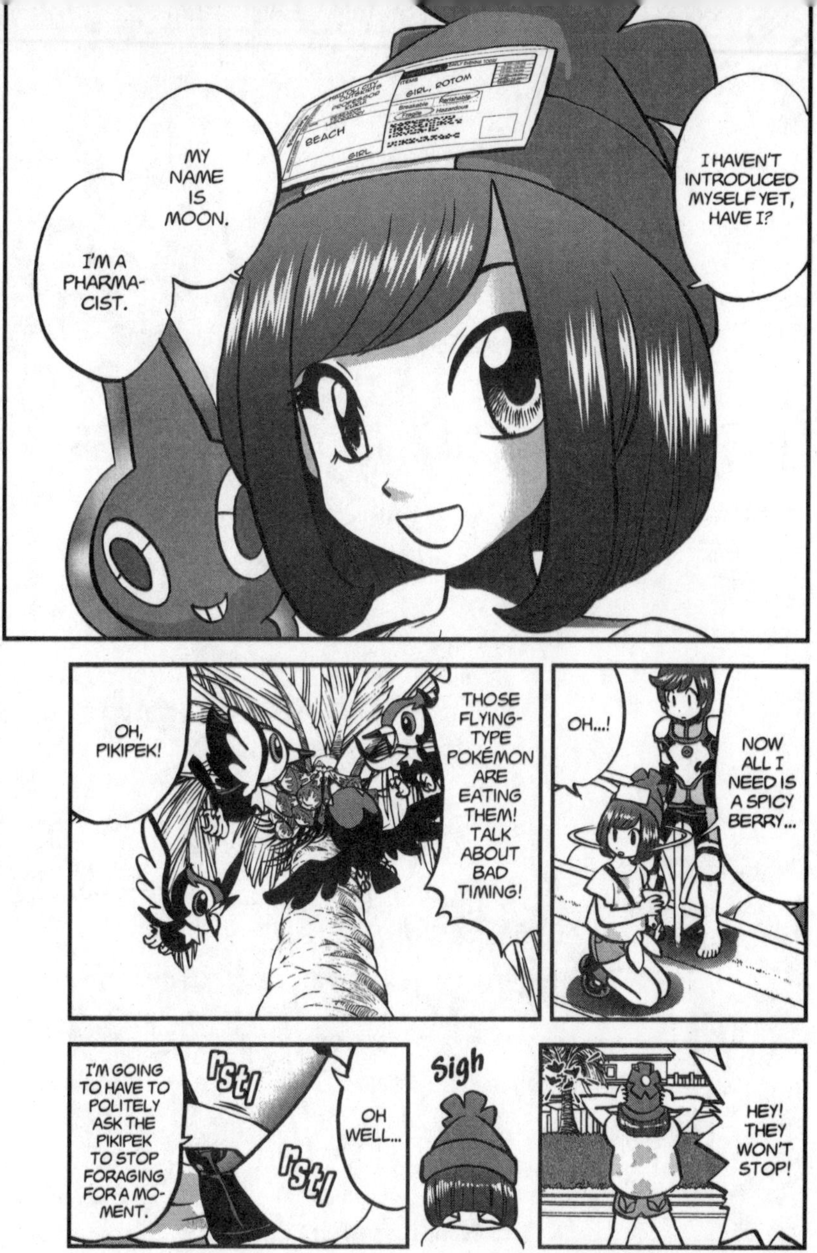
ITEMS
GIRL, ROTOM
Breakable
Perishable
Fragile
Hazardous
BEACH
GIRL
I HAVEN'T INTRODUCED MYSELF YET, HAVE I?
MY NAME IS MOON.
I'M A PHARMA-CIST.
NOW ALL I NEED IS A SPICY BERRY...
OH...!
THOSE FLYING-TYPE POKÉMON ARE EATING THEM! TALK ABOUT BAD TIMING!
OH, PIKIPEK!
HEY! THEY WON'T STOP!
Sigh
OH WELL...
rstl
rstl
I'M GOING TO HAVE TO POLITELY ASK THE PIKIPEK TO STOP FORAGING FOR A MO-MENT.

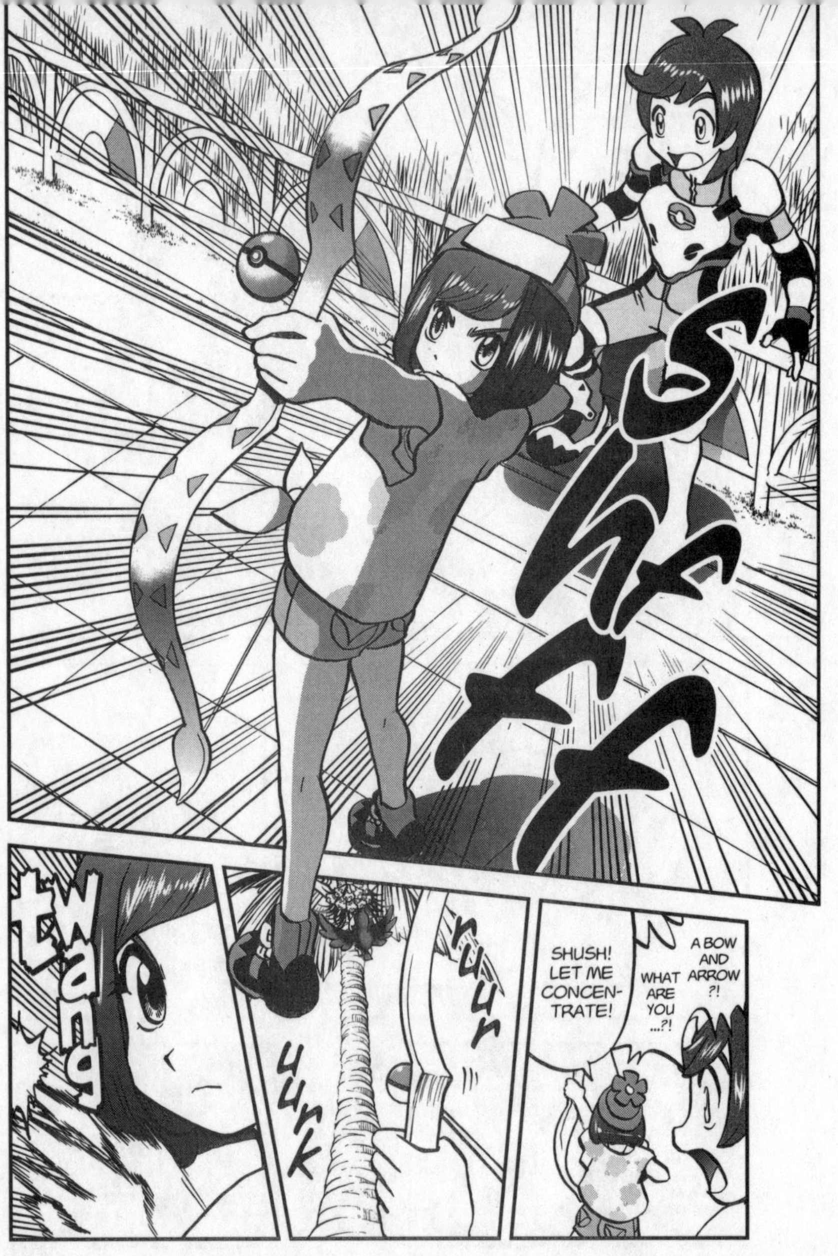

Shfff
A BOW AND ARROW ?!
WHAT ARE YOU ...?!
SHUSH! LET ME CONCEN-TRATE!
ruur
uurk
twang

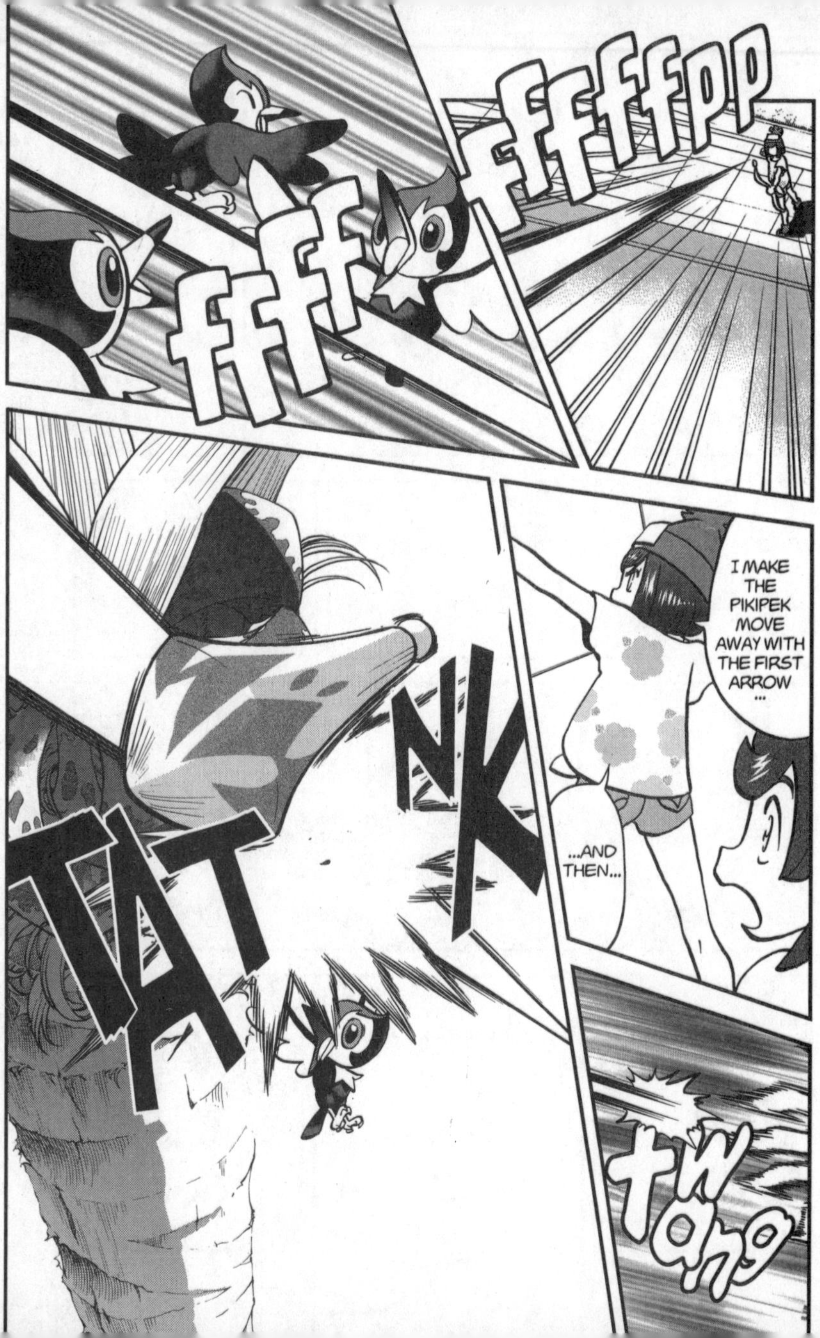
ffffpp
ffff
I MAKE THE PIKIPEK MOVE AWAY WITH THE FIRST ARROW ...
...AND THEN...
TATNK
ftwang

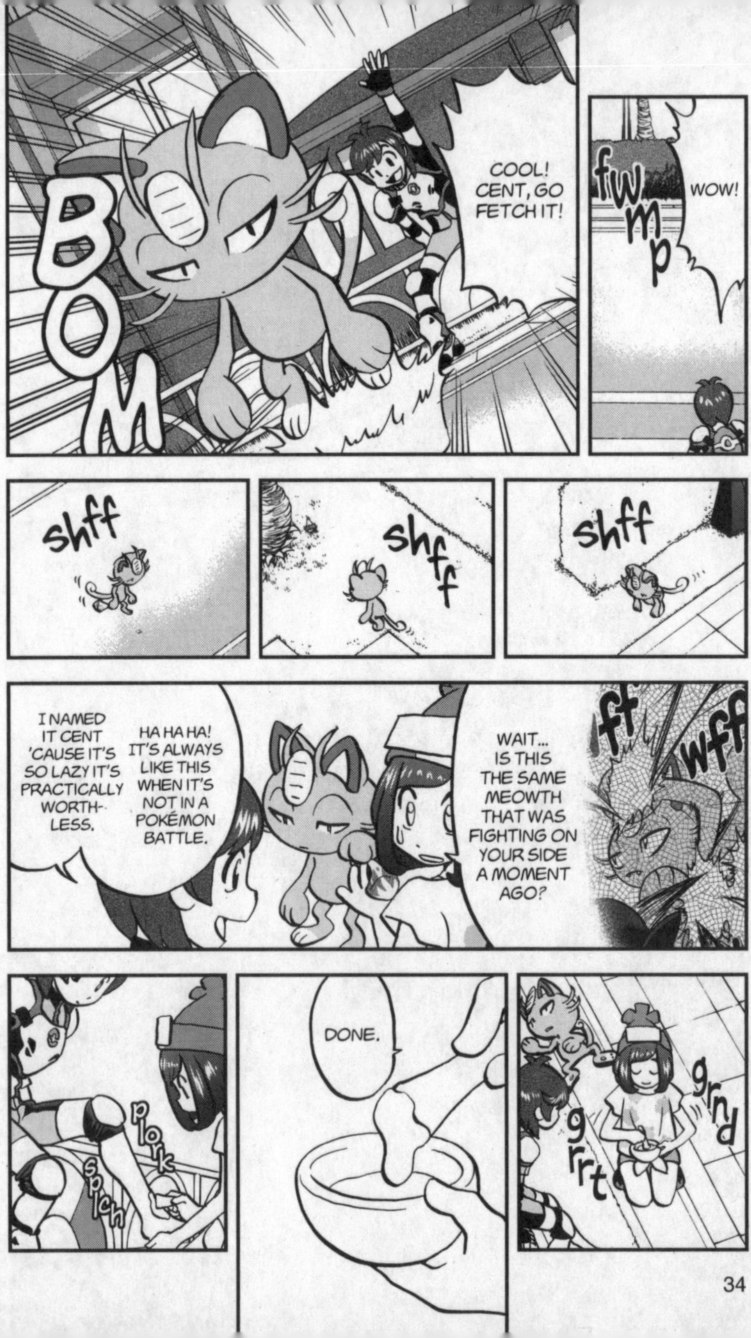
fwmp
WOW!
COOL! CENT, GO FETCH IT!
BOOM
shff
shfff
shff
ff
wff
WAIT... IS THIS THE SAME MEOWTH THAT WAS FIGHTING ON YOUR SIDE A MOMENT AGO?
HA HA HA! IT'S ALWAYS LIKE THIS WHEN IT'S NOT IN A POKÉMON BATTLE.
I NAMED IT CENT 'CAUSE IT'S SO LAZY IT'S PRACTICALLY WORTH-LESS.
grnd
grrt
DONE.
plork
splch

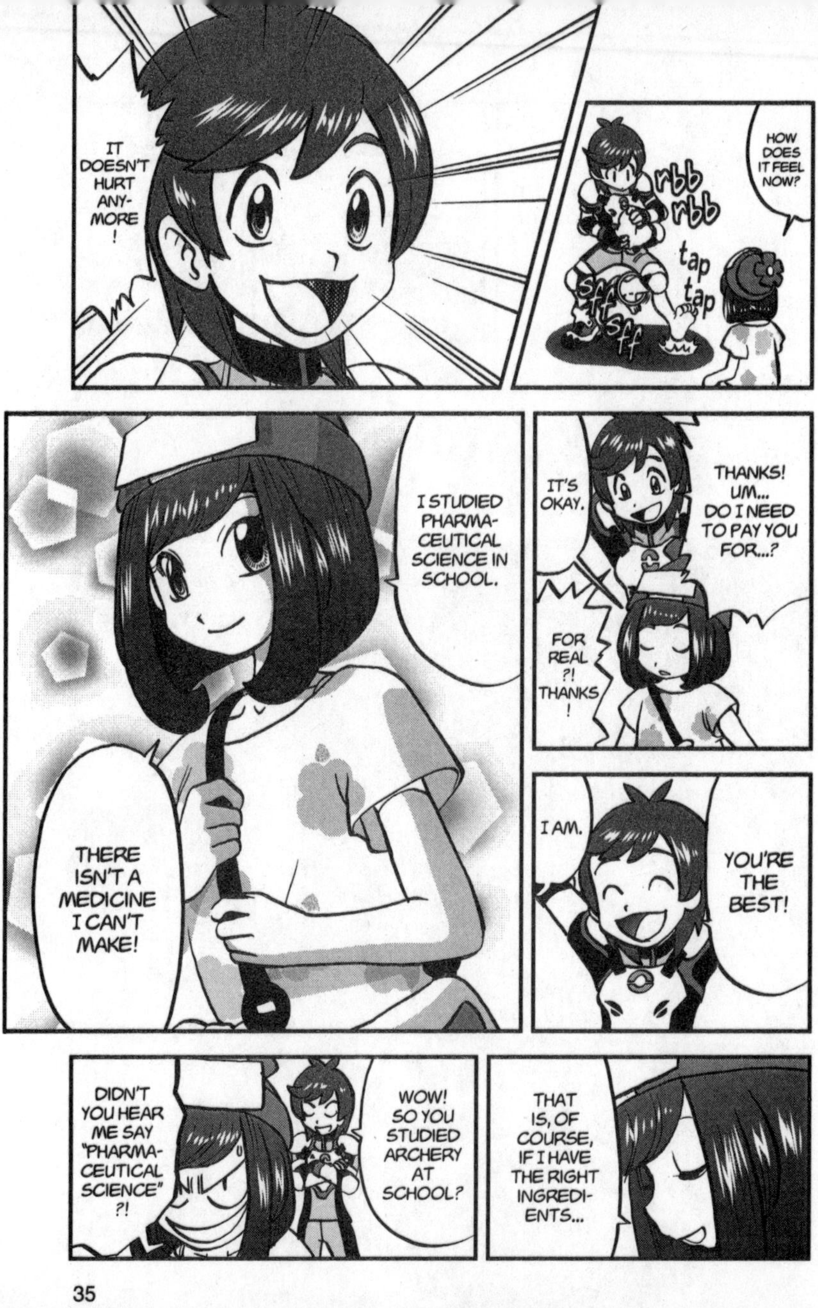
HOW DOES IT FEEL NOW?
rbb rbb
tap tap
sff sff
IT DOESN'T HURT ANY-MORE!
THANKS! UM... DO I NEED TO PAY YOU FOR...?
IT'S OKAY.
FOR REAL?! THANKS!
YOU'RE THE BEST!
I AM.
I STUDIED PHARMA-CEUTICAL SCIENCE IN SCHOOL.
THERE ISN'T A MEDICINE I CAN'T MAKE!
THAT IS, OF COURSE, IF I HAVE THE RIGHT INGREDI-ENTS...
WOW! SO YOU STUDIED ARCHERY AT SCHOOL?
DIDN'T YOU HEAR ME SAY "PHARMA-CEUTICAL SCIENCE"?!

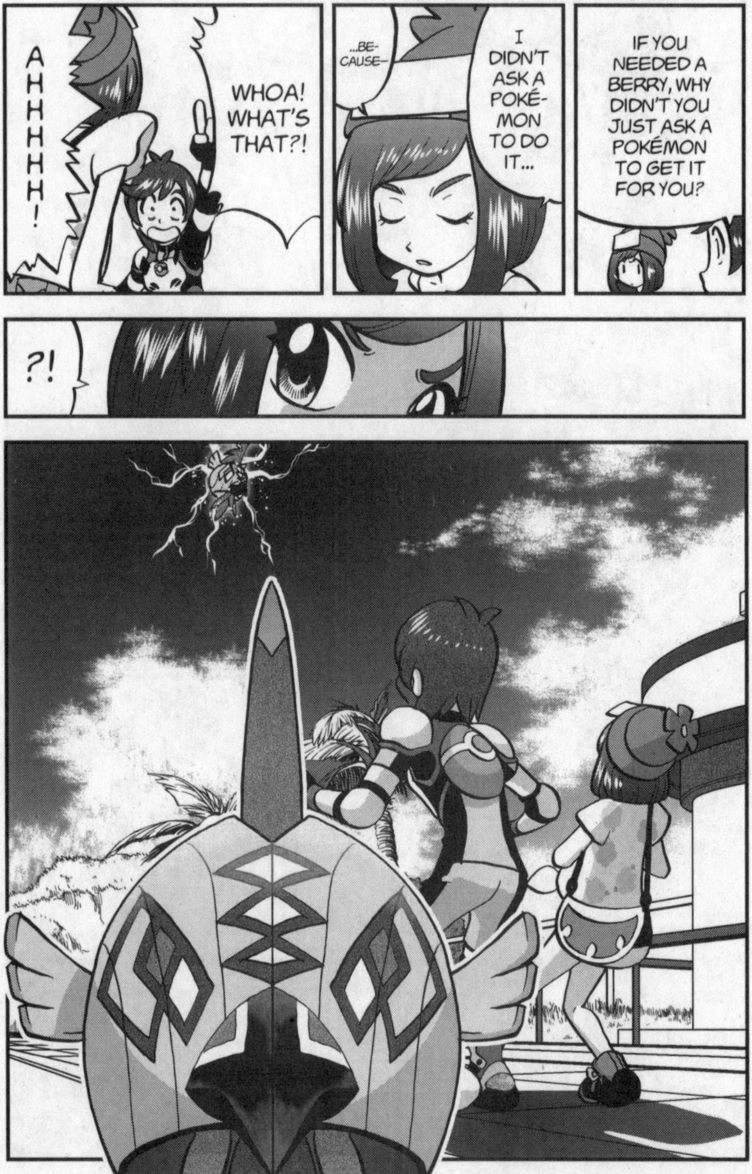
IF YOU NEEDED A BERRY, WHY DIDN'T YOU JUST ASK A POKÉMON TO GET IT FOR YOU?
I DIDN'T ASK A POKÉMON TO DO IT...
...BE-CAUSE—
WHOA! WHAT'S THAT?!
AHHHHHH!
?!

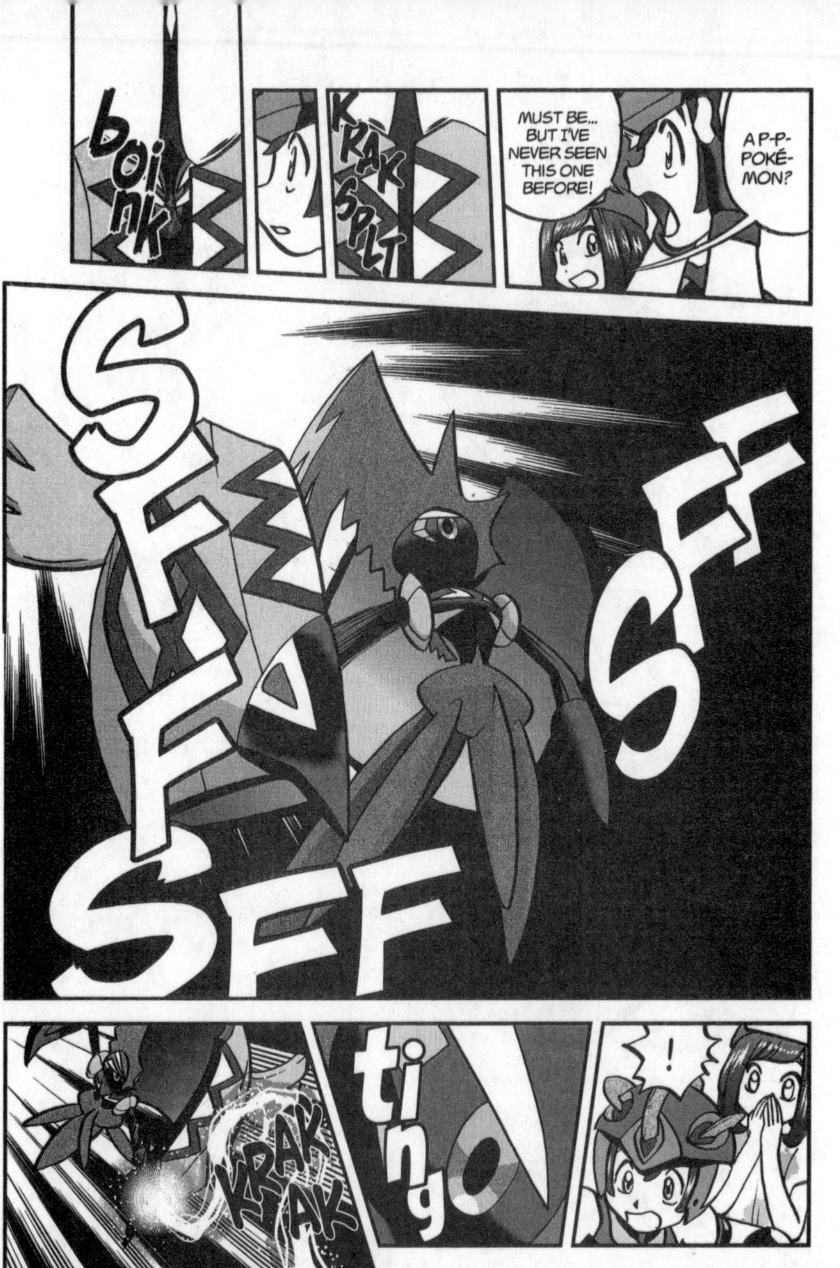

A P-P-POKÉ-MON?
MUST BE... BUT I'VE NEVER SEEN THIS ONE BEFORE!
KRAK SPLT
boink
SFF
SFF
SFF
!
ting
KRAK KRAK

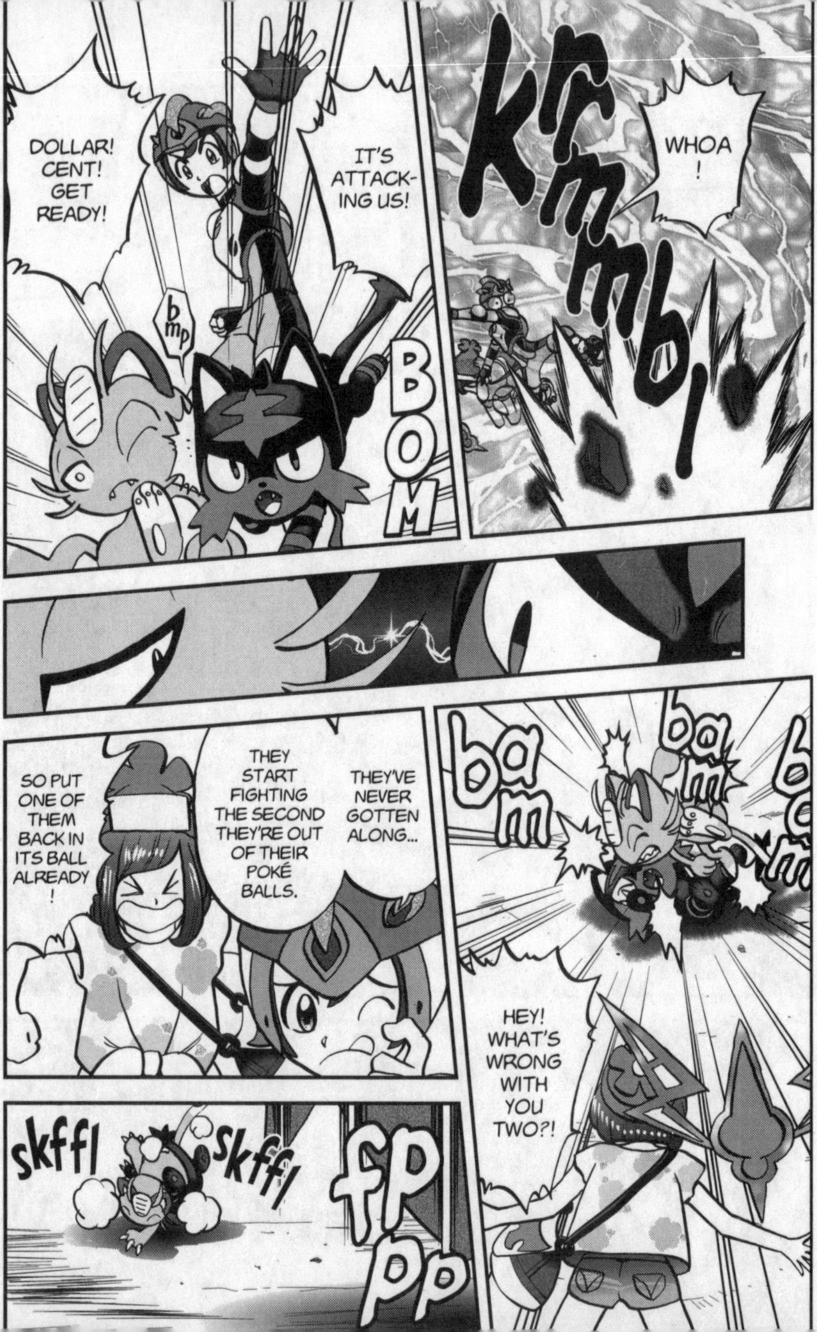
krmmbl!
WHOA!
IT'S ATTACKING US!
DOLLAR! CENT! GET READY!
bmp
BOM
bam
bam
bam
HEY! WHAT'S WRONG WITH YOU TWO?!
THEY'VE NEVER GOTTEN ALONG...
THEY START FIGHTING THE SECOND THEY'RE OUT OF THEIR POKÉ BALLS.
SO PUT ONE OF THEM BACK IN ITS BALL ALREADY!
fp
pp
skffl
skffl

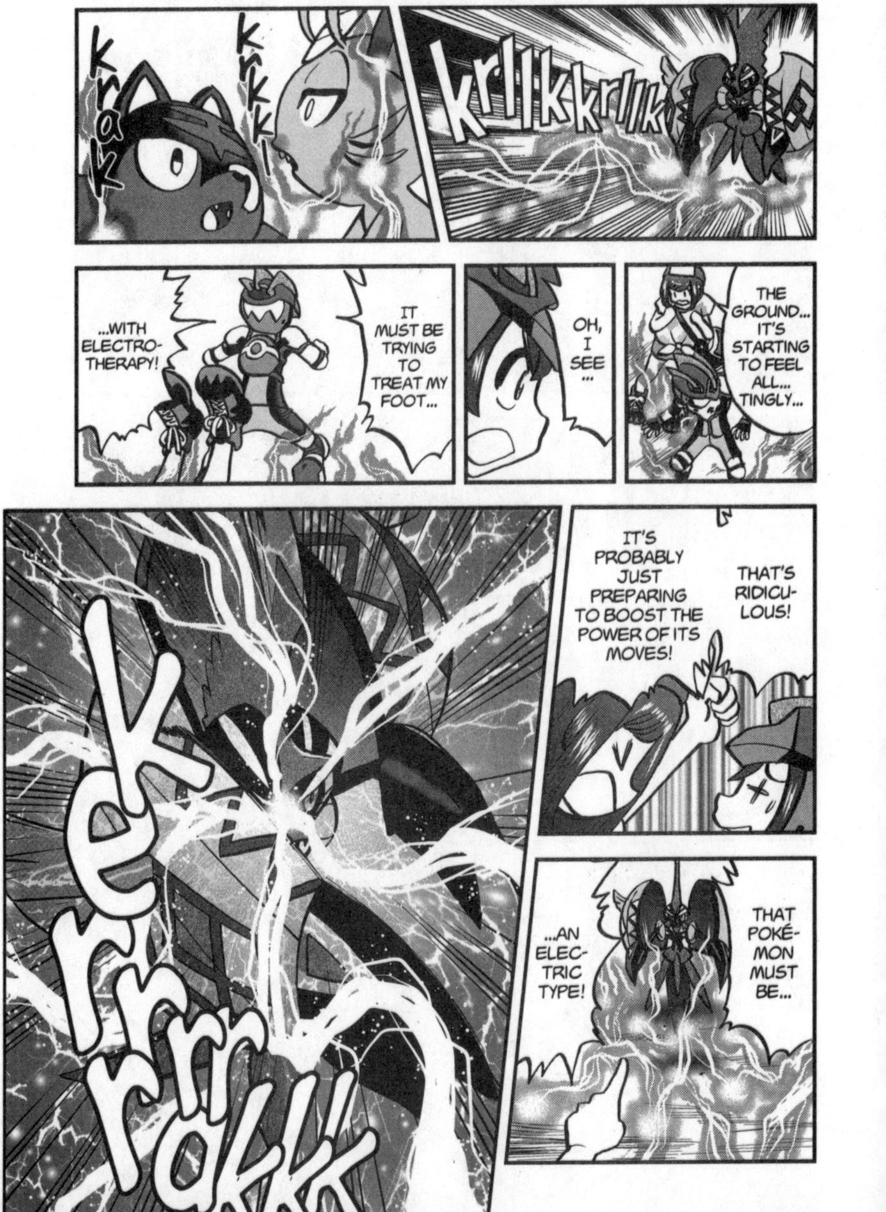
krllkkrllk
krkkk
krakk
THE GROUND... IT'S STARTING TO FEEL ALL... TINGLY...
OH, I SEE...
IT MUST BE TRYING TO TREAT MY FOOT...
...WITH ELECTRO-THERAPY!
THAT'S RIDICU-LOUS!
IT'S PROBABLY JUST PREPARING TO BOOST THE POWER OF ITS MOVES!
THAT POKÉ-MON MUST BE...
...AN ELEC-TRIC TYPE!
ekrrrrrakkk

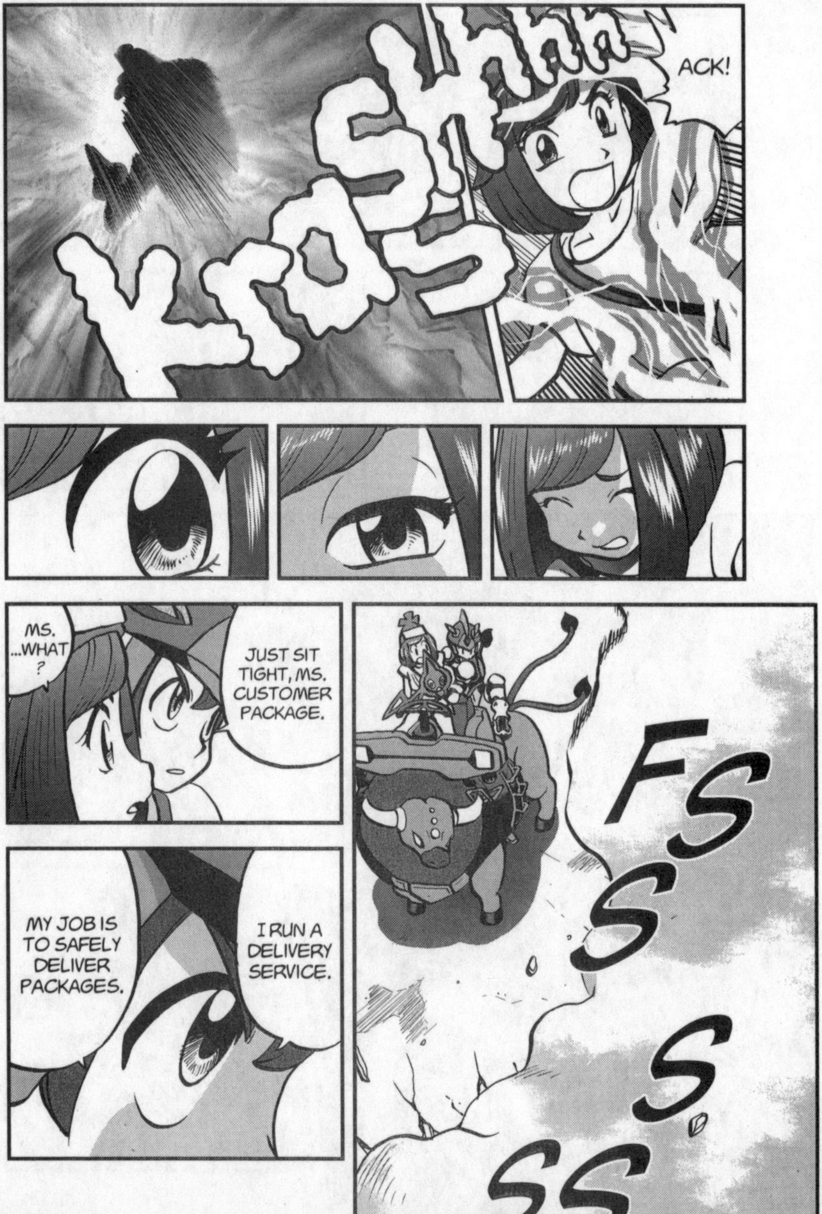
ACK!
KRASSHHH
FSSSSSS
JUST SIT TIGHT, MS. CUSTOMER PACKAGE.
MS. ...WHAT?
I RUN A DELIVERY SERVICE.
MY JOB IS TO SAFELY DELIVER PACKAGES.

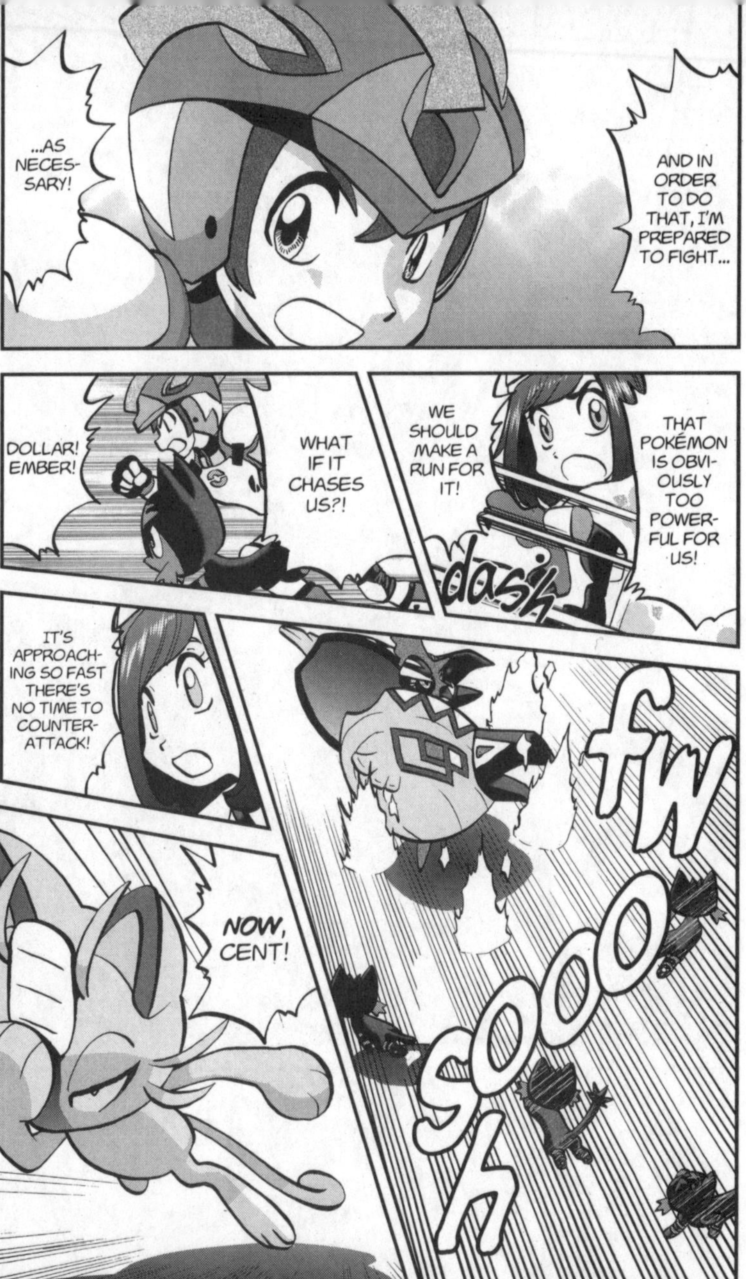

AND IN ORDER TO DO THAT, I'M PREPARED TO FIGHT...
...AS NECES-SARY!
THAT POKÉMON IS OBVI-OUSLY TOO POWER-FUL FOR US!
WE SHOULD MAKE A RUN FOR IT!
dash
WHAT IF IT CHASES US?!
DOLLAR! EMBER!
fw
SOOOOSh
IT'S APPROACH-ING SO FAST THERE'S NO TIME TO COUNTER-ATTACK!
NOW, CENT!

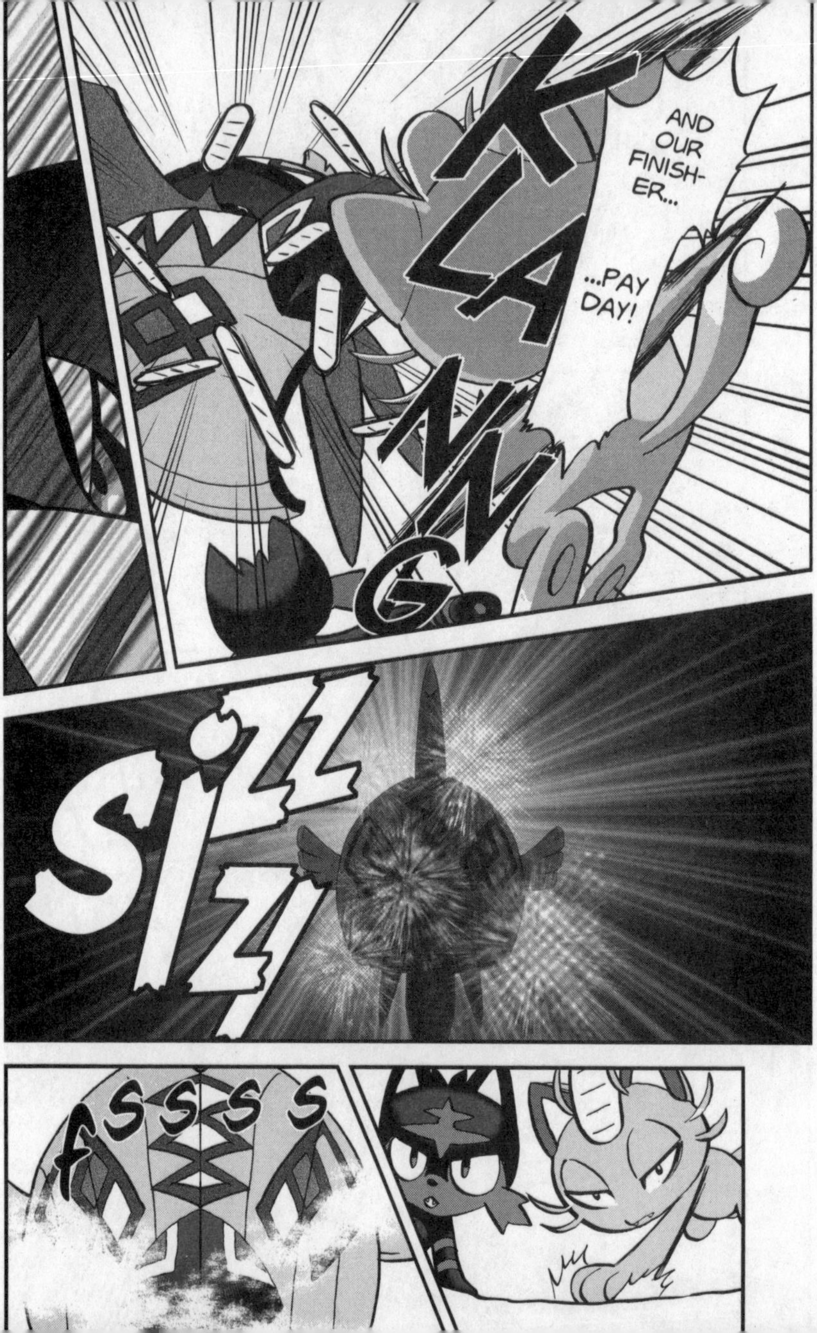
AND OUR FINISHER...
...PAY DAY!
KLANNG
SIZZZ
FSSSSS

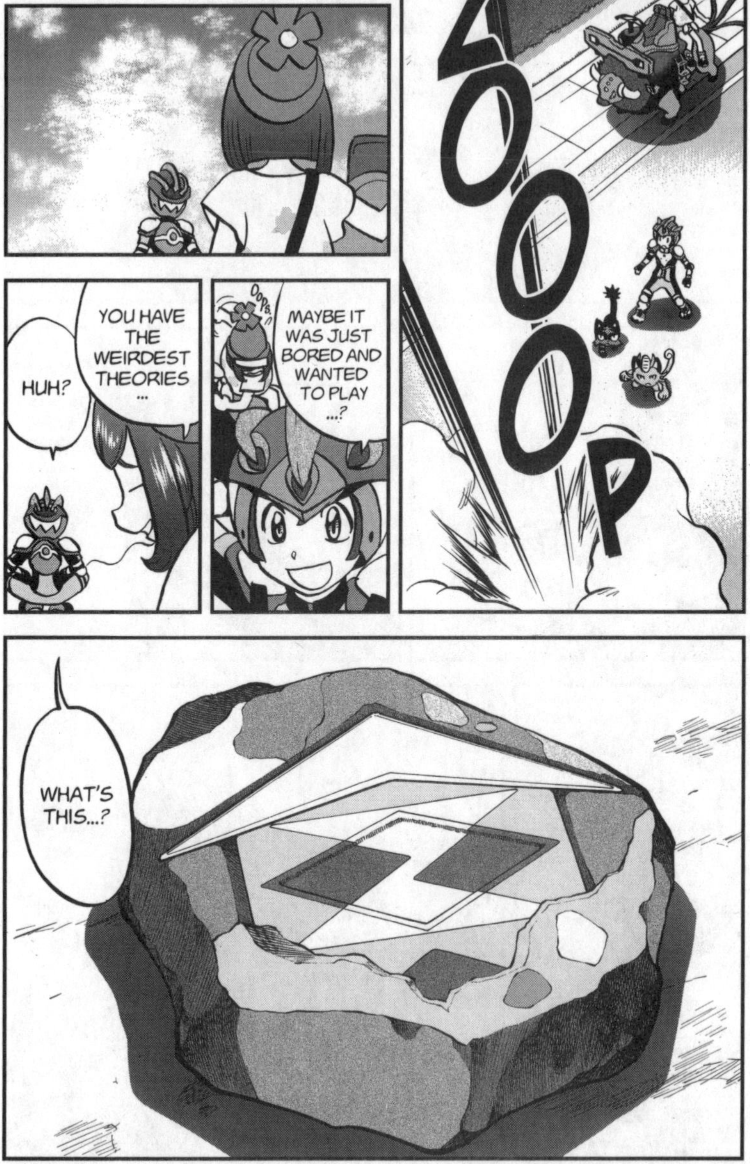
ZOOOOOP
OOPS.
MAYBE IT WAS JUST BORED AND WANTED TO PLAY ...?
YOU HAVE THE WEIRDEST THEORIES ...
HUH?
WHAT'S THIS...?

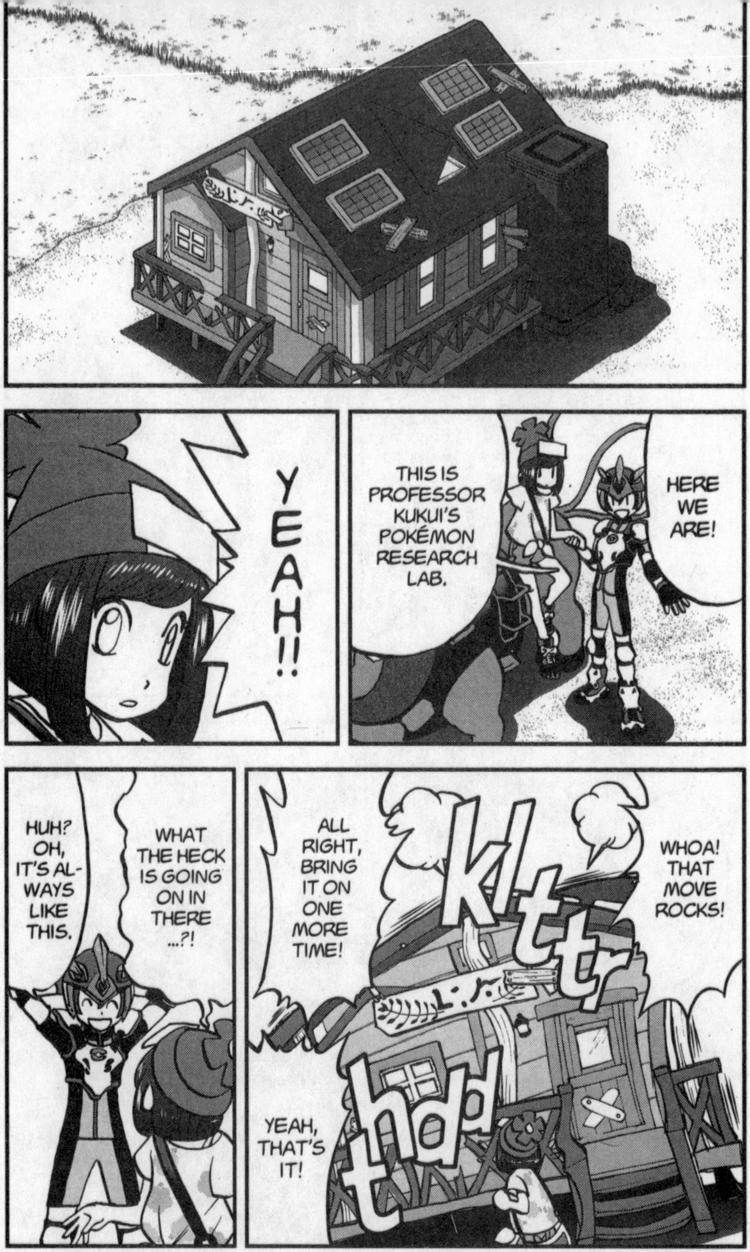
HERE WE ARE!
THIS IS PROFESSOR KUKUI'S POKÉMON RESEARCH LAB.
YEAH!!
WHOA! THAT MOVE ROCKS!
klttr
ALL RIGHT, BRING IT ON ONE MORE TIME!
hddt
YEAH, THAT'S IT!
WHAT THE HECK IS GOING ON IN THERE ...?!
HUH? OH, IT'S AL-WAYS LIKE THIS.

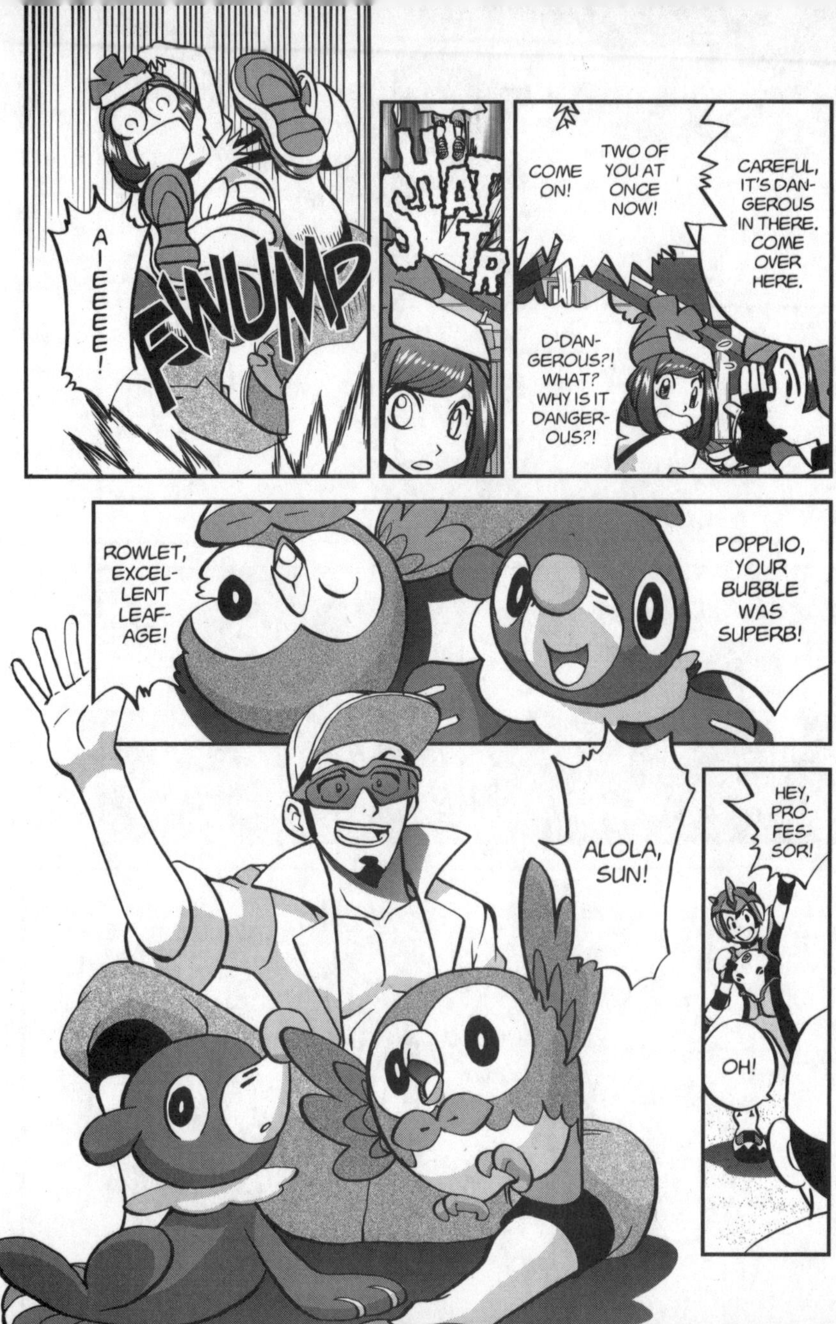

CAREFUL, IT'S DANGEROUS IN THERE. COME OVER HERE.
TWO OF YOU AT ONCE NOW!
COME ON!
D-DANGEROUS?! WHAT? WHY IS IT DANGEROUS?!
SHATTR
AIEEEE!
FWUMP
POPPLIO, YOUR BUBBLE WAS SUPERB!
ROWLET, EXCELLENT LEAFAGE!
HEY, PROFESSOR!
OH!
ALOLA, SUN!

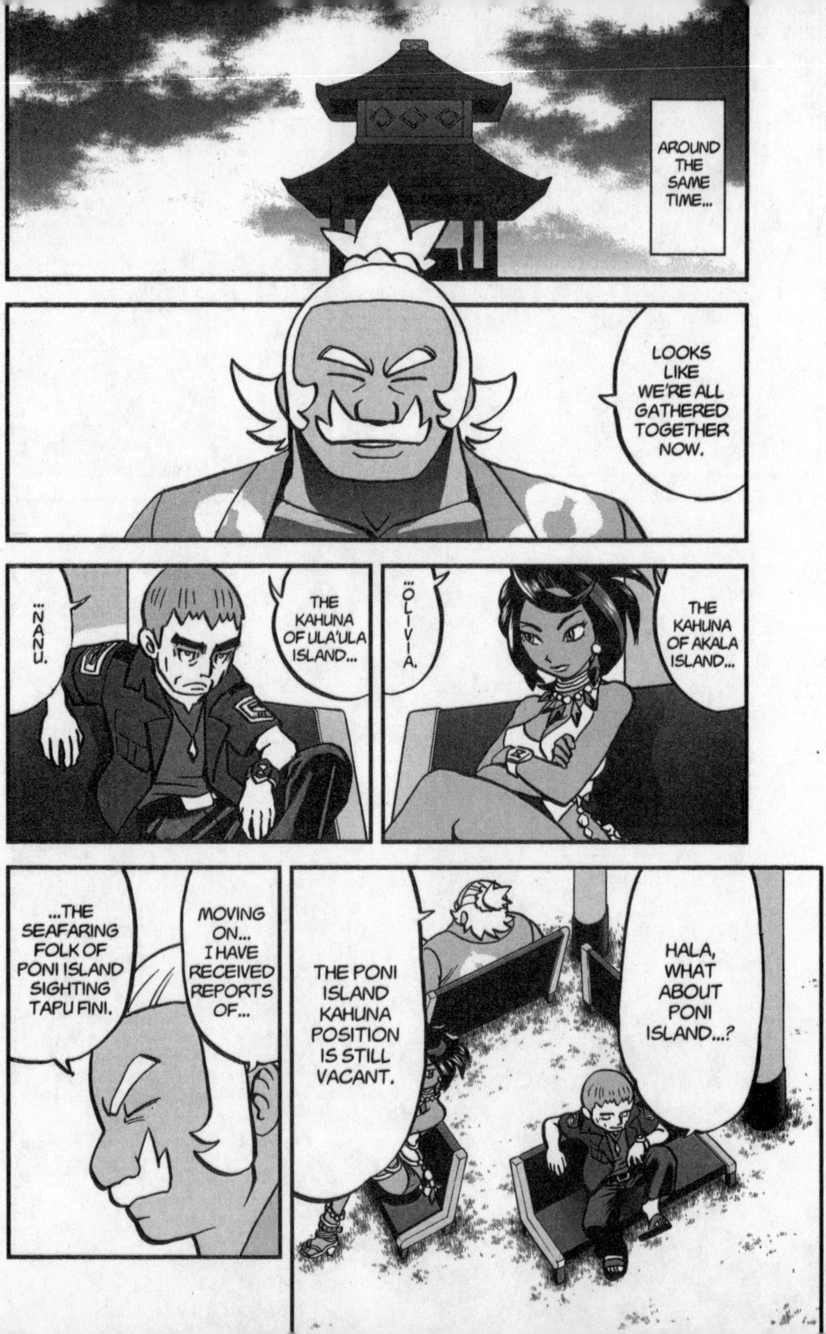
AROUND THE SAME TIME...
LOOKS LIKE WE'RE ALL GATHERED TOGETHER NOW.
THE KAHUNA OF AKALA ISLAND...
...OLIVIA.
THE KAHUNA OF ULA'ULA ISLAND...
...NANU.
HALA, WHAT ABOUT PONI ISLAND...?
THE PONI ISLAND KAHUNA POSITION IS STILL VACANT.
MOVING ON... I HAVE RECEIVED REPORTS OF...
...THE SEAFARING FOLK OF PONI ISLAND SIGHTING TAPU FINI.

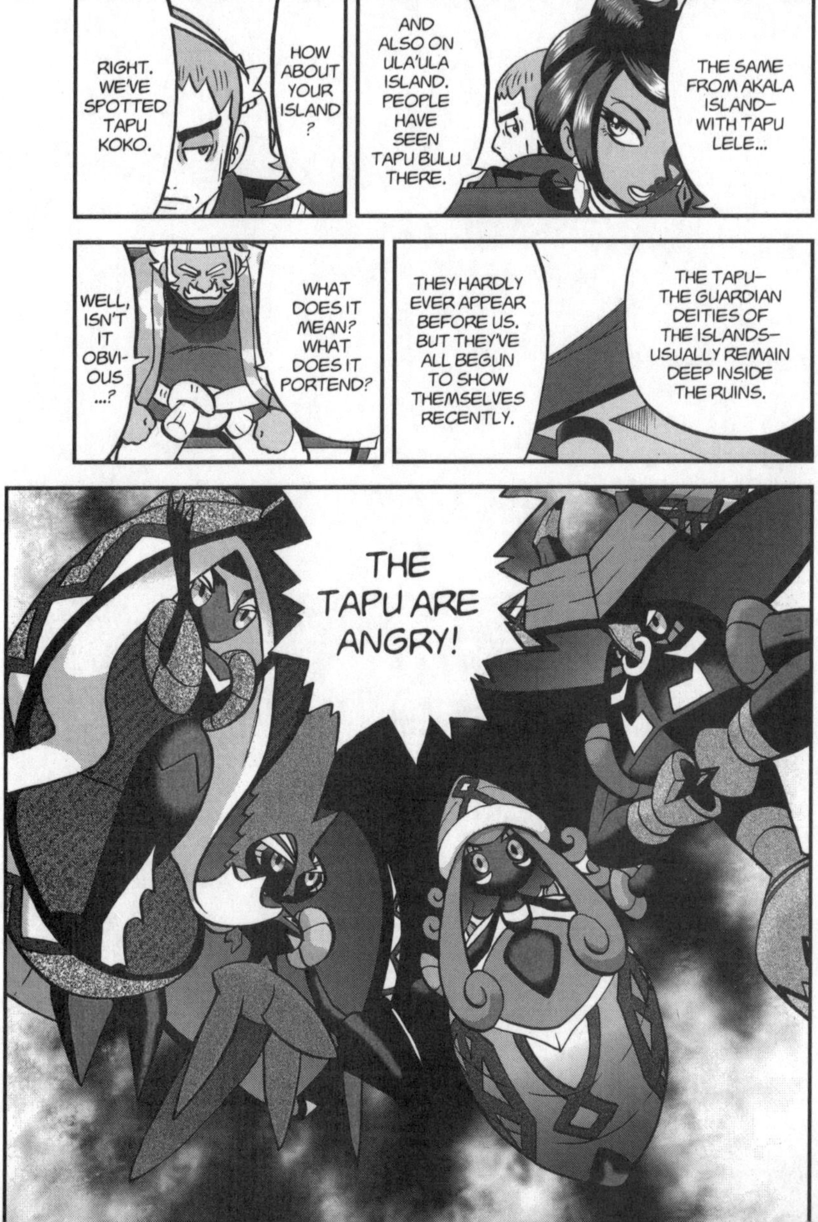
THE SAME FROM AKALA ISLAND— WITH TAPU LELE...
AND ALSO ON ULA'ULA ISLAND. PEOPLE HAVE SEEN TAPU BULU THERE.
HOW ABOUT YOUR ISLAND?
RIGHT. WE'VE SPOTTED TAPU KOKO.
THE TAPU— THE GUARDIAN DEITIES OF THE ISLANDS— USUALLY REMAIN DEEP INSIDE THE RUINS.
THEY HARDLY EVER APPEAR BEFORE US. BUT THEY'VE ALL BEGUN TO SHOW THEMSELVES RECENTLY.
WHAT DOES IT MEAN? WHAT DOES IT PORTEND?
WELL, ISN'T IT OBVIOUS...?
THE TAPU ARE ANGRY!

A Comfey Greeting

It is a tradition on Alola to greet
tourists from other regions with a lei,
a necklace made of flowers.
But beware! That lei might turn out to be
a Comfey, a Flower-type Pokémon!
It's just a harmless little
mischief-maker though.

Guide to Alola 2

Adventure 3
Pokémon Move Specialist Professor Kukui

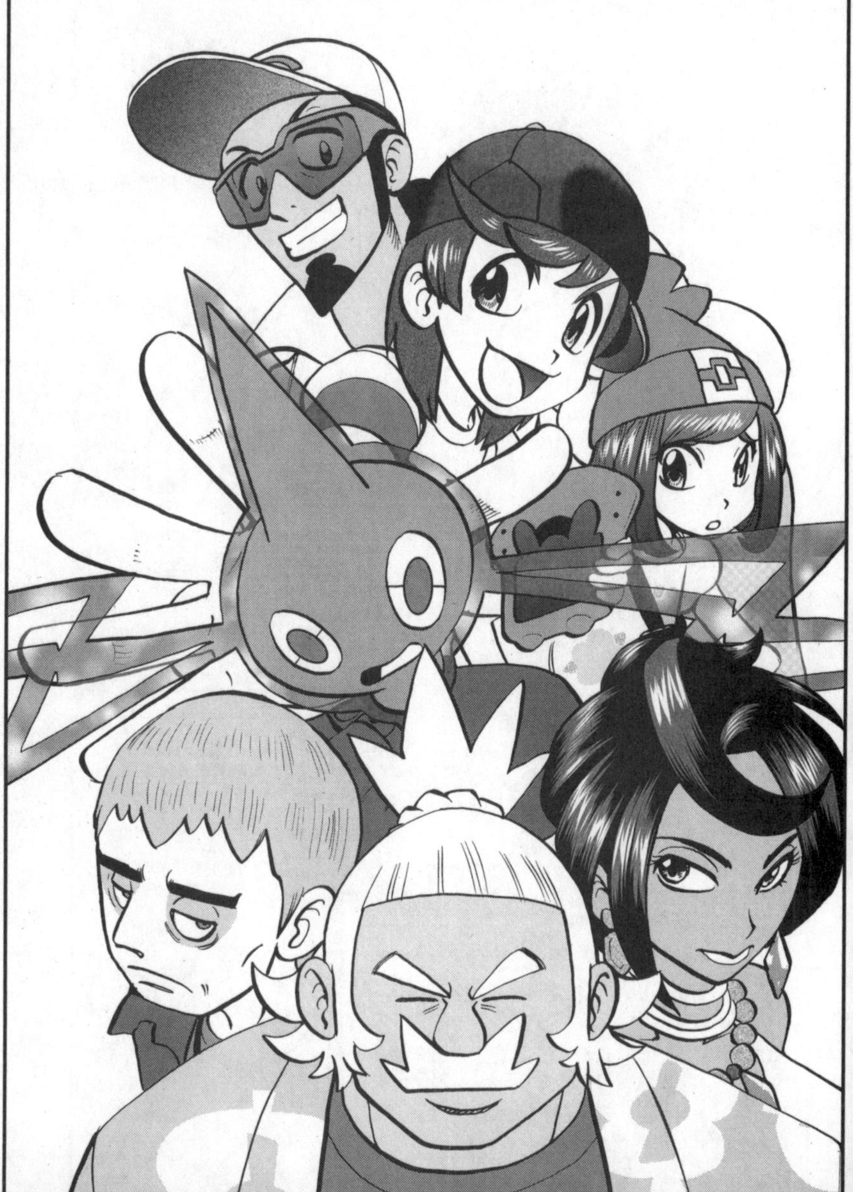

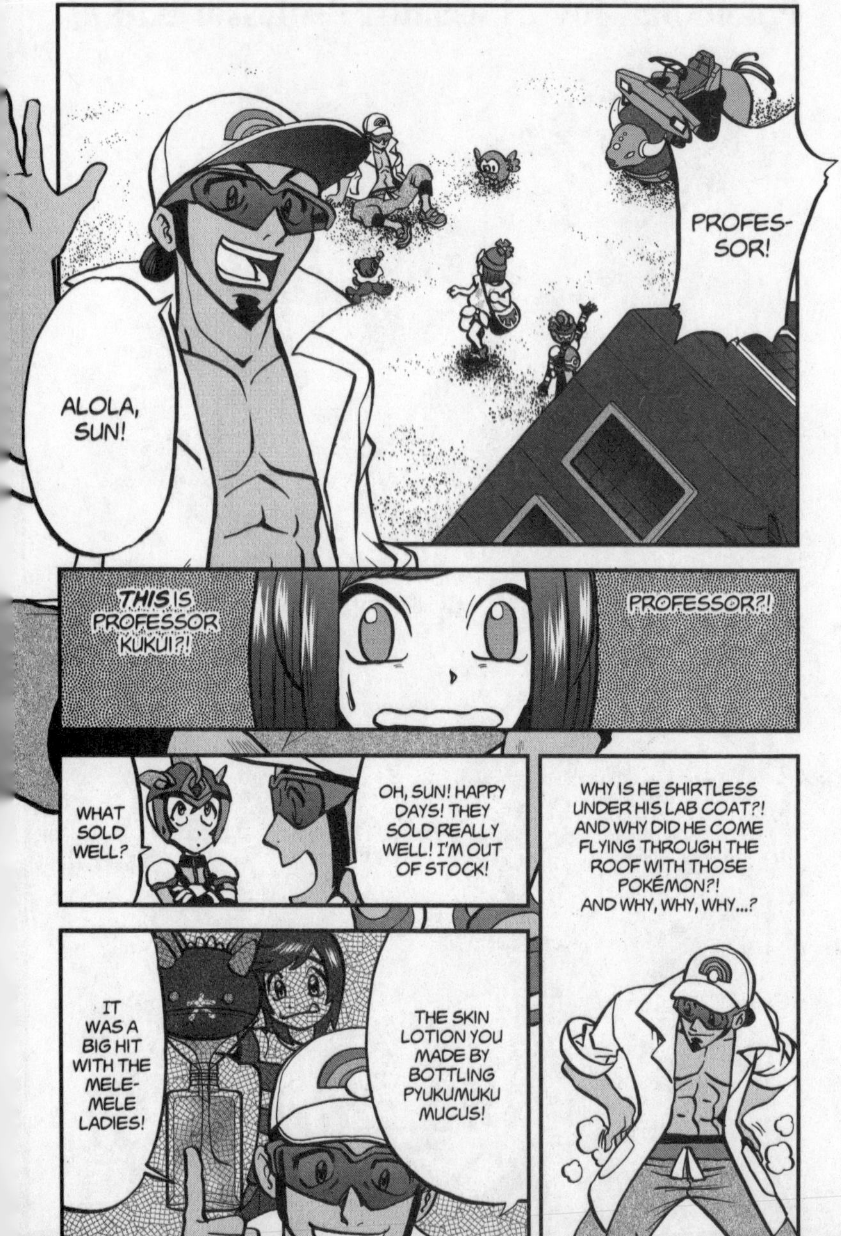
PROFES-SOR!
ALOLA, SUN!
PROFESSOR?!
THIS IS PROFESSOR KUKUI?!
WHY IS HE SHIRTLESS UNDER HIS LAB COAT?! AND WHY DID HE COME FLYING THROUGH THE ROOF WITH THOSE POKÉMON?! AND WHY, WHY, WHY...?
OH, SUN! HAPPY DAYS! THEY SOLD REALLY WELL! I'M OUT OF STOCK!
WHAT SOLD WELL?
THE SKIN LOTION YOU MADE BY BOTTLING PYUKUMUKU MUCUS!
IT WAS A BIG HIT WITH THE MELE-MELE LADIES!

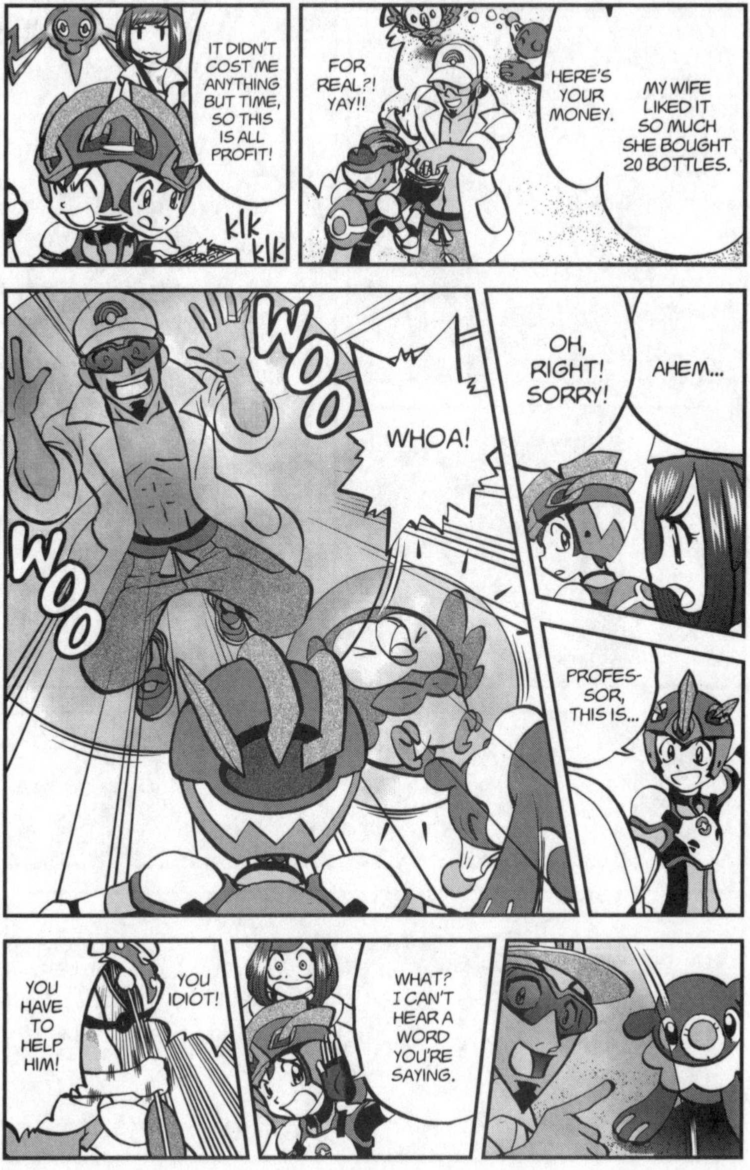
MY WIFE LIKED IT SO MUCH SHE BOUGHT 20 BOTTLES.
HERE'S YOUR MONEY.
FOR REAL?! YAY!!
IT DIDN'T COST ME ANYTHING BUT TIME, SO THIS IS ALL PROFIT!
klk klk
AHEM...
OH, RIGHT! SORRY!
PROFES-SOR, THIS IS...
WHOA!
WOO WOO
WOO WOO
WHAT? I CAN'T HEAR A WORD YOU'RE SAYING.
YOU IDIOT!
YOU HAVE TO HELP HIM!

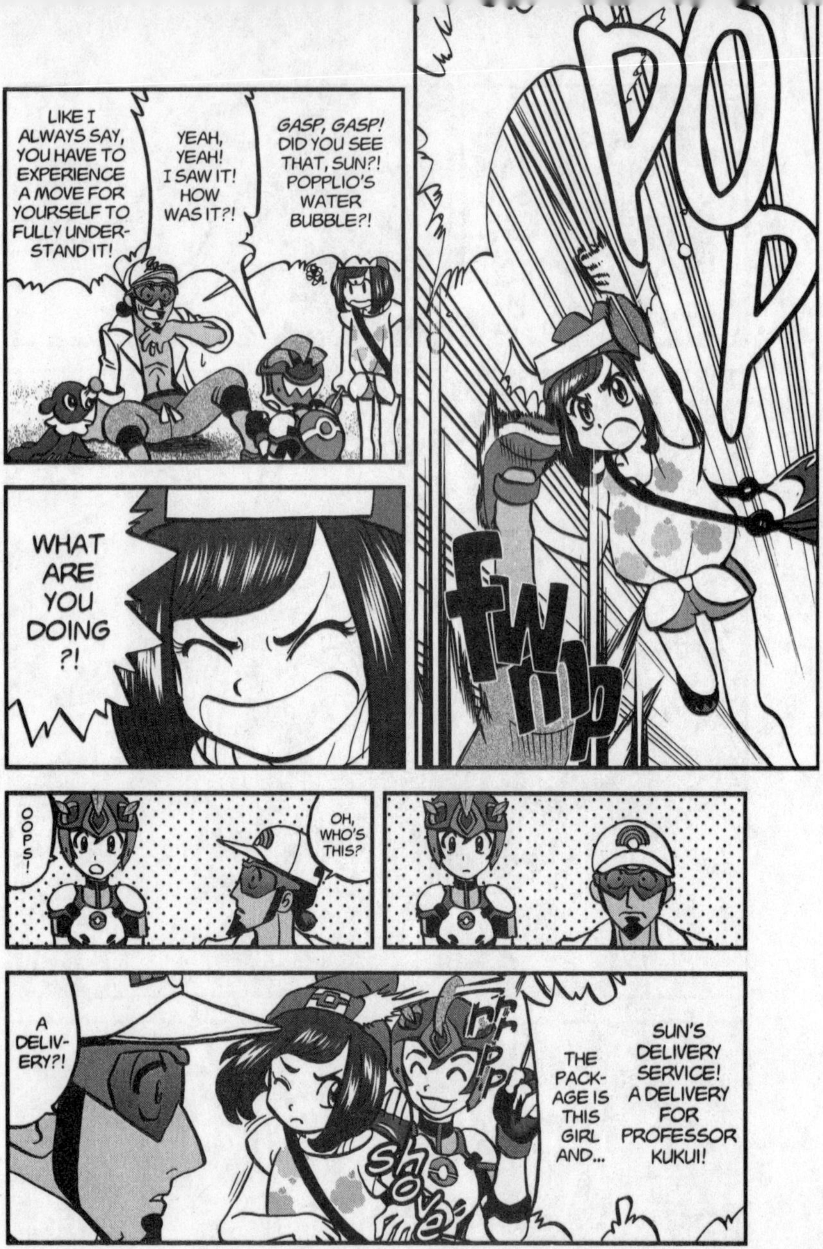

POP
FWOOP
GASP, GASP! DID YOU SEE THAT, SUN?! POPPLIO'S WATER BUBBLE?!
YEAH, YEAH! I SAW IT! HOW WAS IT?!
LIKE I ALWAYS SAY, YOU HAVE TO EXPERIENCE A MOVE FOR YOURSELF TO FULLY UNDER-STAND IT!
WHAT ARE YOU DOING?!
OH, WHO'S THIS?
OOPS!
SUN'S DELIVERY SERVICE! A DELIVERY FOR PROFESSOR KUKUI!
THE PACK-AGE IS THIS GIRL AND...
shove
A DELIV-ERY?!

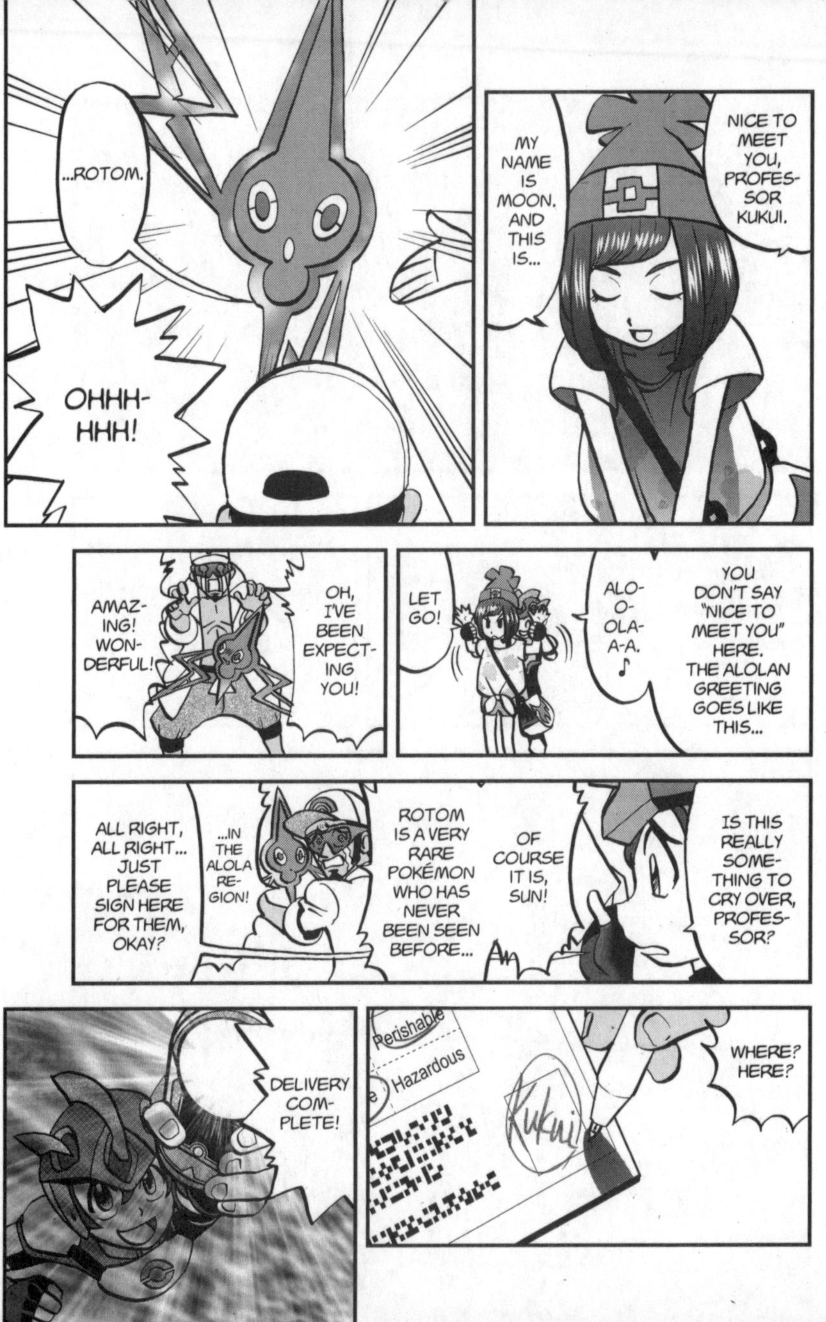
NICE TO MEET YOU, PROFESSOR KUKUI.
MY NAME IS MOON. AND THIS IS...
...ROTOM.
OHHH-HHH!
YOU DON'T SAY "NICE TO MEET YOU" HERE. THE ALOLAN GREETING GOES LIKE THIS...
ALO-O-OLA-A-A. ♪
LET GO!
OH, I'VE BEEN EXPECTING YOU!
AMAZING! WONDERFUL!
IS THIS REALLY SOMETHING TO CRY OVER, PROFESSOR?
OF COURSE IT IS, SUN!
ROTOM IS A VERY RARE POKÉMON WHO HAS NEVER BEEN SEEN BEFORE...
...IN THE ALOLA REGION!
ALL RIGHT, ALL RIGHT... JUST PLEASE SIGN HERE FOR THEM, OKAY?
WHERE? HERE?
Perishable
Hazardous
Kukui
DELIVERY COMPLETE!

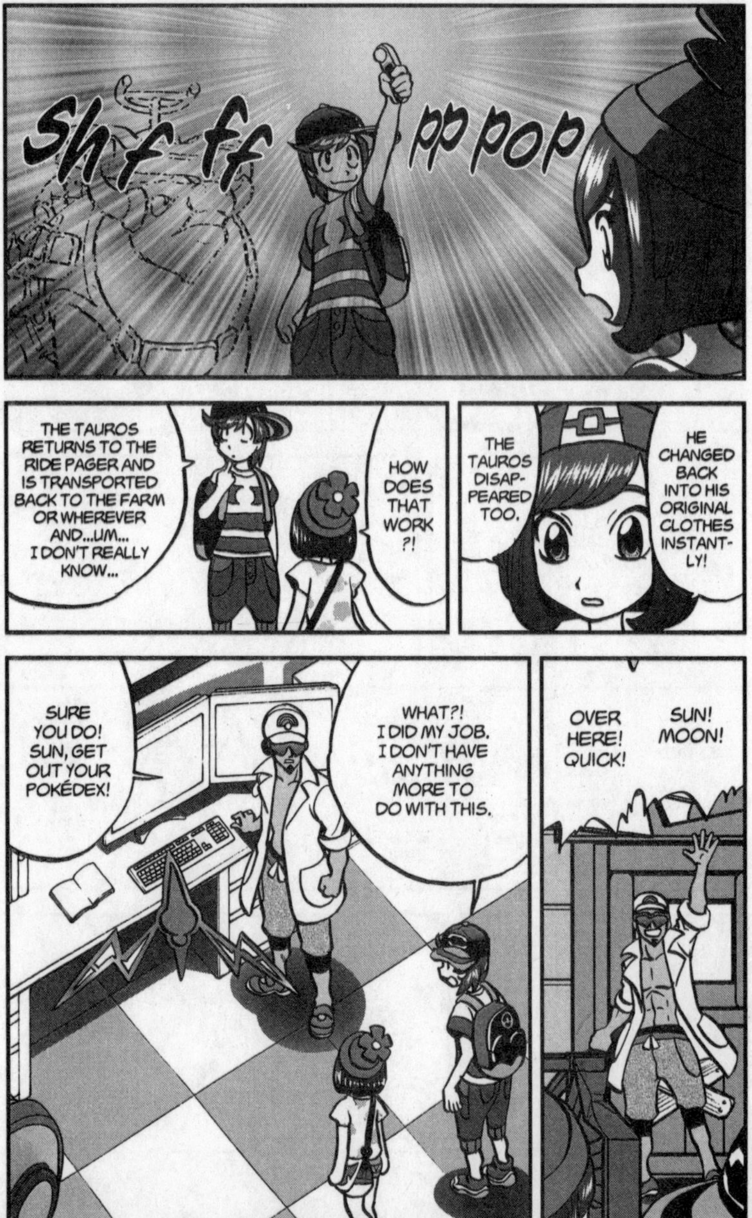
pp pop
Shf ff
HE CHANGED BACK INTO HIS ORIGINAL CLOTHES INSTANT-LY!
THE TAUROS DISAP-PEARED TOO.
HOW DOES THAT WORK ?!
THE TAUROS RETURNS TO THE RIDE PAGER AND IS TRANSPORTED BACK TO THE FARM OR WHEREVER AND...UM... I DON'T REALLY KNOW...
SUN! MOON!
OVER HERE! QUICK!
WHAT?! I DID MY JOB. I DON'T HAVE ANYTHING MORE TO DO WITH THIS.
SURE YOU DO! SUN, GET OUT YOUR POKÉDEX!

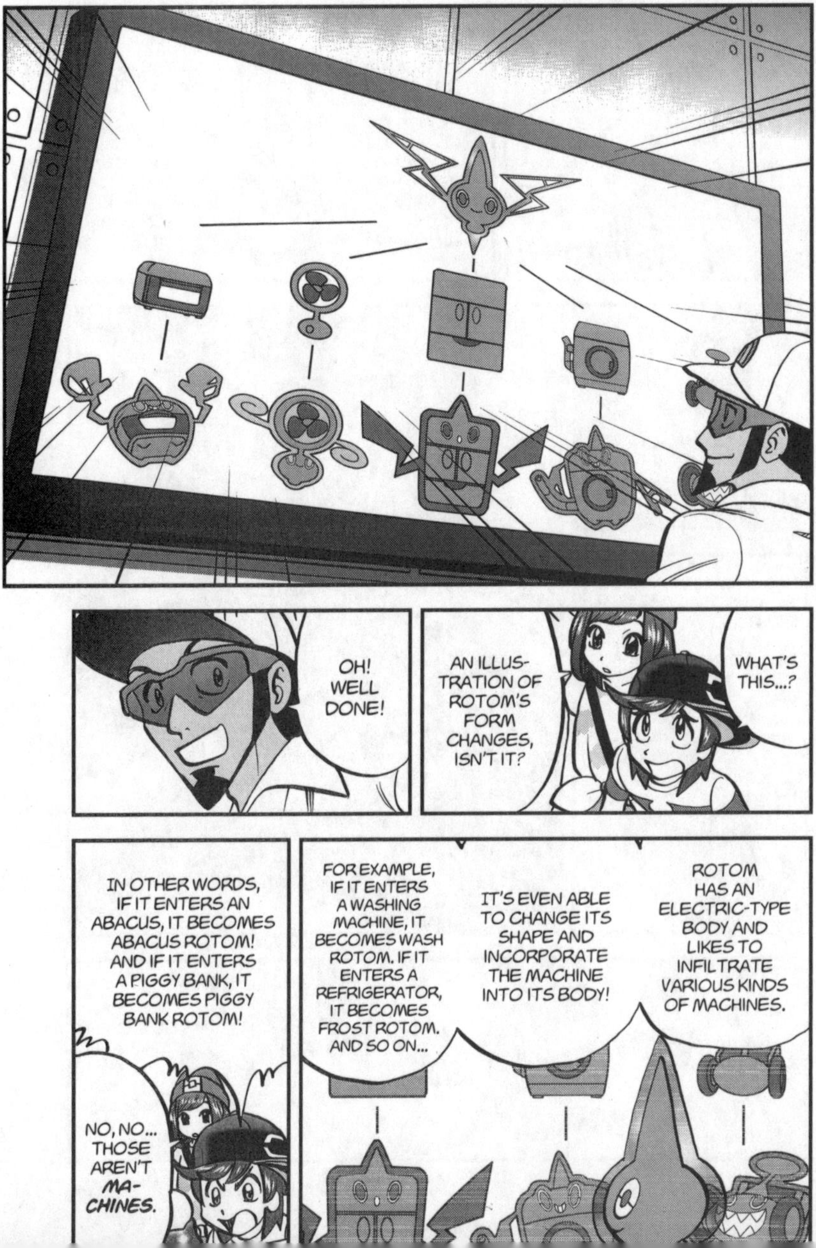
WHAT'S THIS...?
AN ILLUSTRATION OF ROTOM'S FORM CHANGES, ISN'T IT?
OH! WELL DONE!
ROTOM HAS AN ELECTRIC-TYPE BODY AND LIKES TO INFILTRATE VARIOUS KINDS OF MACHINES.
IT'S EVEN ABLE TO CHANGE ITS SHAPE AND INCORPORATE THE MACHINE INTO ITS BODY!
FOR EXAMPLE, IF IT ENTERS A WASHING MACHINE, IT BECOMES WASH ROTOM. IF IT ENTERS A REFRIGERATOR, IT BECOMES FROST ROTOM. AND SO ON...
IN OTHER WORDS, IF IT ENTERS AN ABACUS, IT BECOMES ABACUS ROTOM! AND IF IT ENTERS A PIGGY BANK, IT BECOMES PIGGY BANK ROTOM!
NO, NO... THOSE AREN'T *MACHINES*.

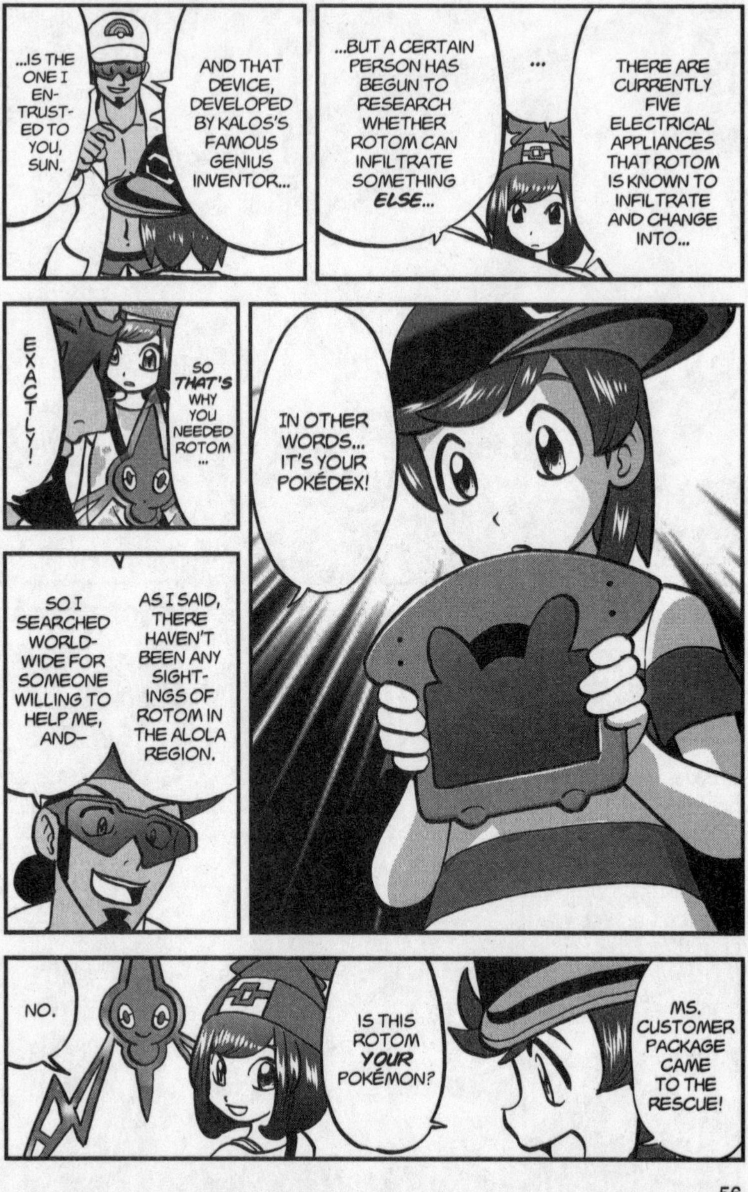
THERE ARE CURRENTLY FIVE ELECTRICAL APPLIANCES THAT ROTOM IS KNOWN TO INFILTRATE AND CHANGE INTO...
...
...BUT A CERTAIN PERSON HAS BEGUN TO RESEARCH WHETHER ROTOM CAN INFILTRATE SOMETHING *ELSE*...
AND THAT DEVICE, DEVELOPED BY KALOS'S FAMOUS GENIUS INVENTOR...
...IS THE ONE I EN-TRUST-ED TO YOU, SUN.
IN OTHER WORDS... IT'S YOUR POKÉDEX!
SO *THAT'S* WHY YOU NEEDED ROTOM...
EXACTLY!
AS I SAID, THERE HAVEN'T BEEN ANY SIGHT-INGS OF ROTOM IN THE ALOLA REGION.
SO I SEARCHED WORLD-WIDE FOR SOMEONE WILLING TO HELP ME, AND-
MS. CUSTOMER PACKAGE CAME TO THE RESCUE!
IS THIS ROTOM *YOUR* POKÉMON?
NO.

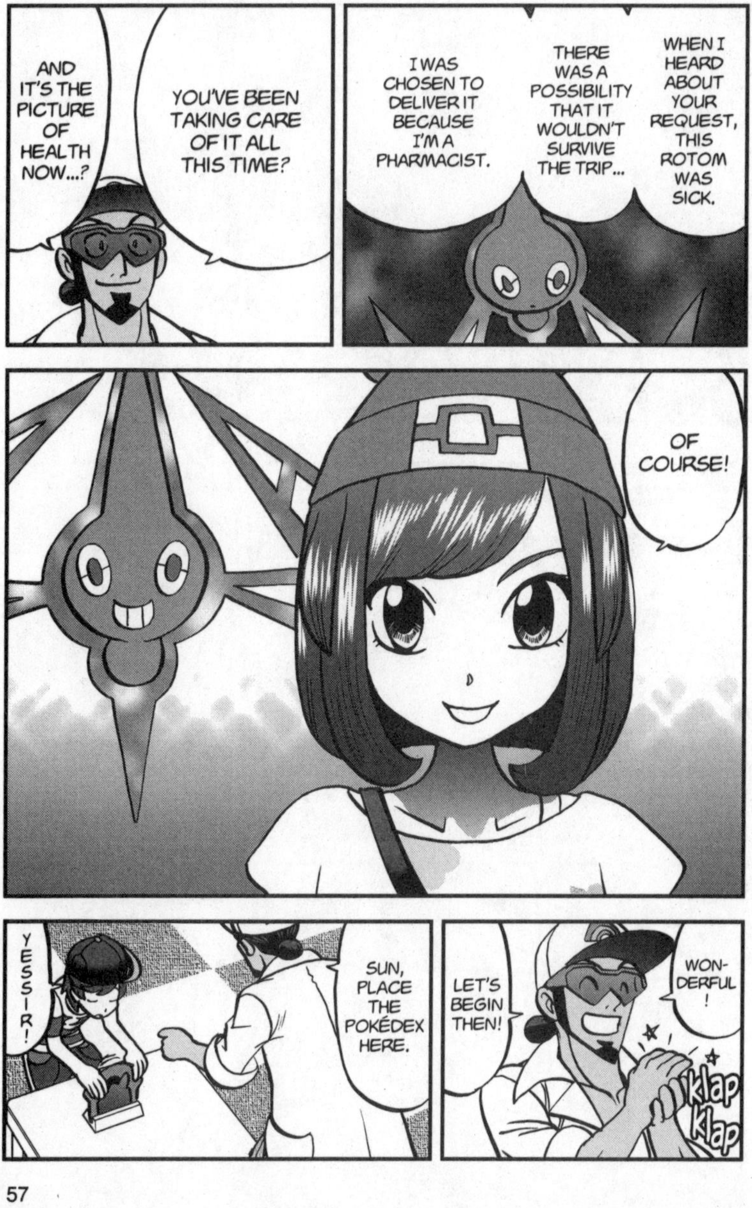
WHEN I HEARD ABOUT YOUR REQUEST, THIS ROTOM WAS SICK.
THERE WAS A POSSIBILITY THAT IT WOULDN'T SURVIVE THE TRIP...
I WAS CHOSEN TO DELIVER IT BECAUSE I'M A PHARMACIST.
YOU'VE BEEN TAKING CARE OF IT ALL THIS TIME?
AND IT'S THE PICTURE OF HEALTH NOW...?
OF COURSE!
WON-DERFUL!
LET'S BEGIN THEN!
klap klap
SUN, PLACE THE POKÉDEX HERE.
YESSIR!

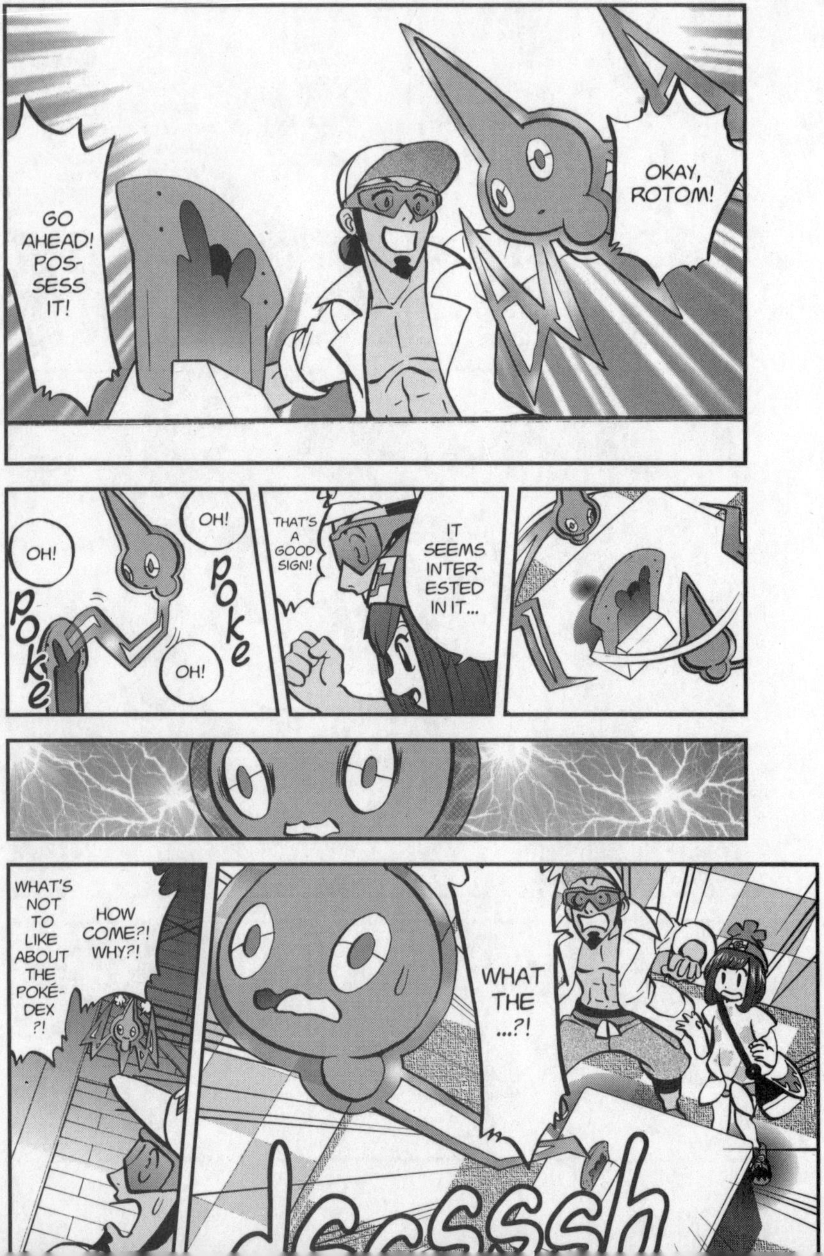
OKAY, ROTOM!
GO AHEAD! POS-SESS IT!
IT SEEMS INTER-ESTED IN IT...
THAT'S A GOOD SIGN!
OH!
OH!
poke
poke
OH!
WHAT THE ...?!
HOW COME?! WHY?!
WHAT'S NOT TO LIKE ABOUT THE POKÉ-DEX?!
desssh

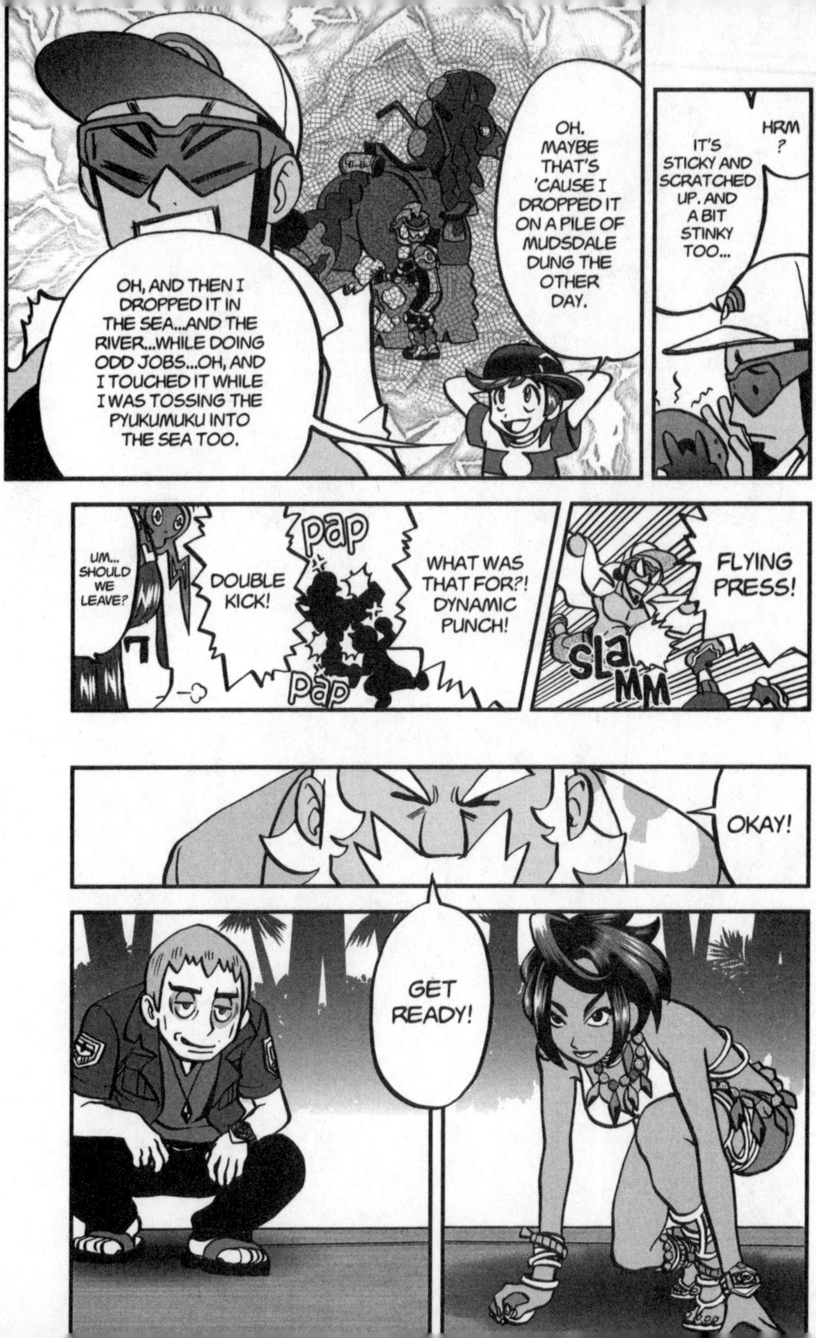
HRM?
IT'S STICKY AND SCRATCHED UP. AND A BIT STINKY TOO...
OH. MAYBE THAT'S 'CAUSE I DROPPED IT ON A PILE OF MUDSDALE DUNG THE OTHER DAY.
OH, AND THEN I DROPPED IT IN THE SEA...AND THE RIVER...WHILE DOING ODD JOBS...OH, AND I TOUCHED IT WHILE I WAS TOSSING THE PYUKUMUKU INTO THE SEA TOO.
FLYING PRESS!
SLAMM
WHAT WAS THAT FOR?! DYNAMIC PUNCH!
pap
DOUBLE KICK!
pap
UM... SHOULD WE LEAVE?
OKAY!
GET READY!

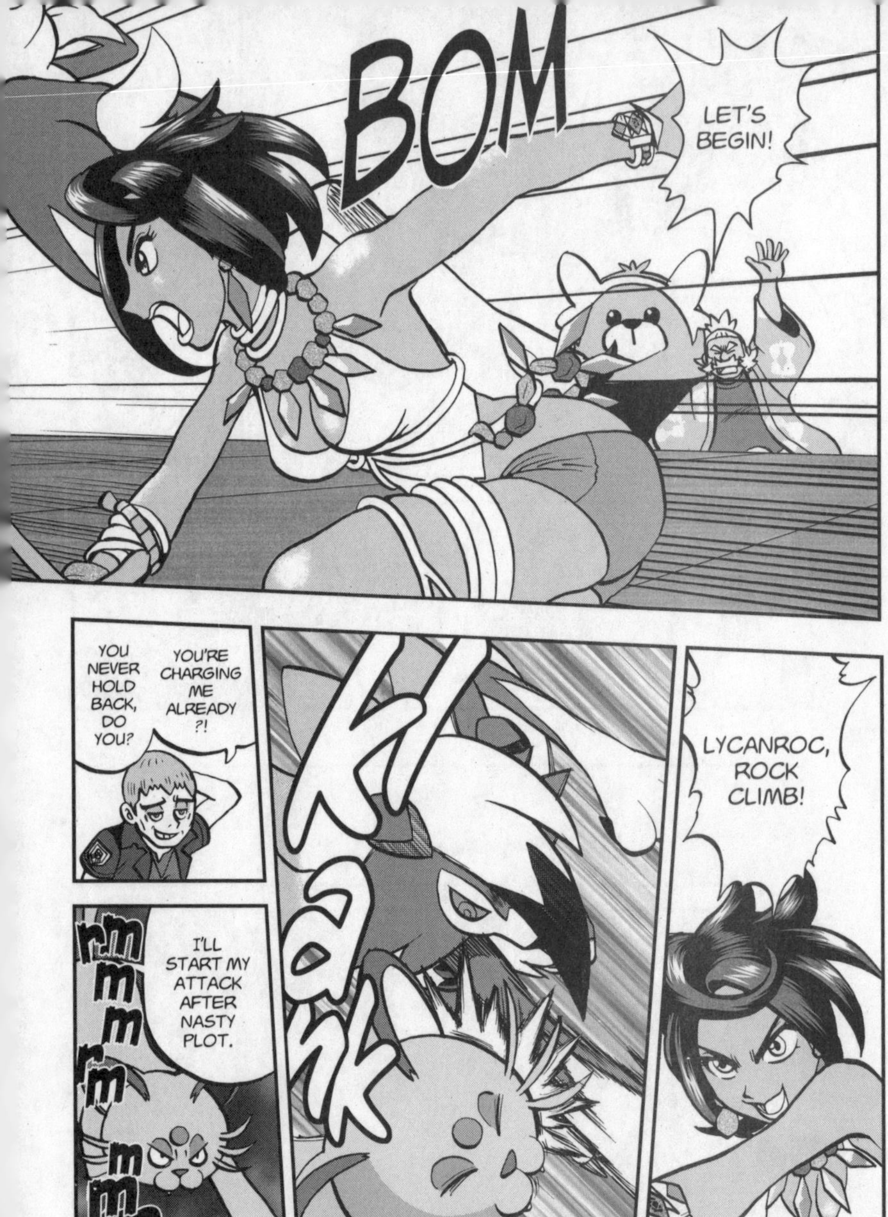
BOM
LET'S BEGIN!
LYCANROC, ROCK CLIMB!
YOU'RE CHARGING ME ALREADY?!
YOU NEVER HOLD BACK, DO YOU?
I'LL START MY ATTACK AFTER NASTY PLOT.

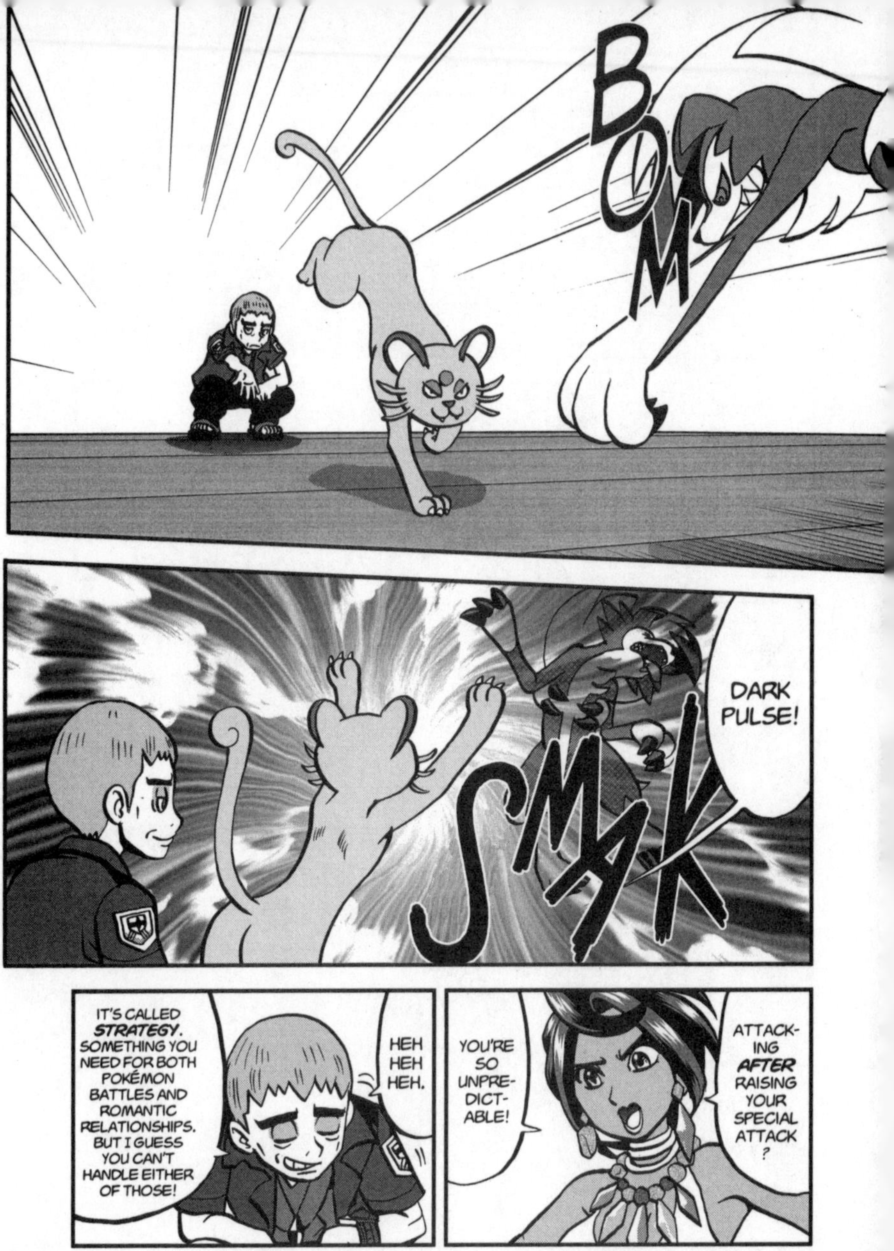
BOOM
DARK PULSE!
SMAK
ATTACK-ING AFTER RAISING YOUR SPECIAL ATTACK?
YOU'RE SO UNPREDICTABLE!
HEH HEH HEH.
IT'S CALLED STRATEGY. SOMETHING YOU NEED FOR BOTH POKÉMON BATTLES AND ROMANTIC RELATIONSHIPS. BUT I GUESS YOU CAN'T HANDLE EITHER OF THOSE!

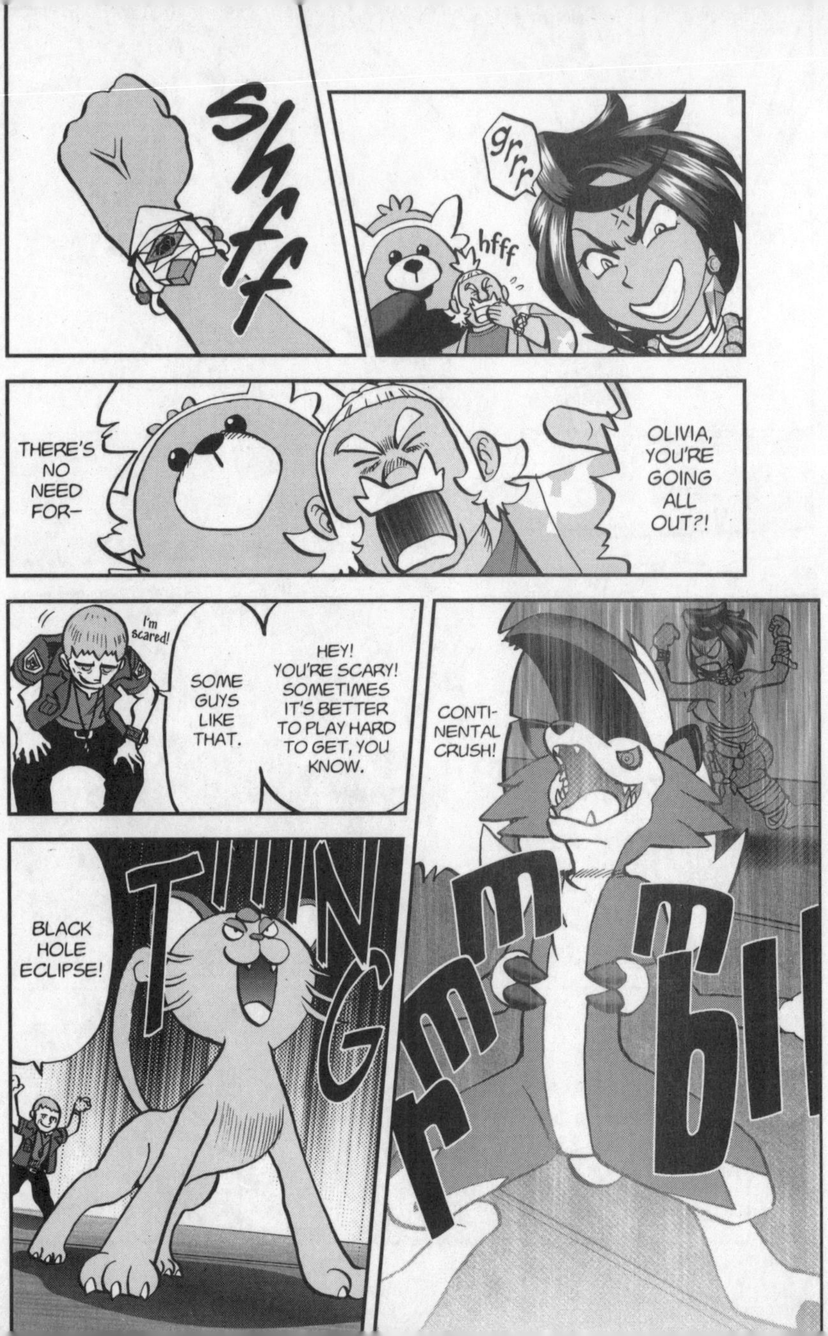
grrr
hfff
shfff
OLIVIA, YOU'RE GOING ALL OUT?!
THERE'S NO NEED FOR–
CONTI-NENTAL CRUSH!
rmmbl
HEY! YOU'RE SCARY! SOMETIMES IT'S BETTER TO PLAY HARD TO GET, YOU KNOW.
SOME GUYS LIKE THAT.
I'm scared!
BLACK HOLE ECLIPSE!
TWING

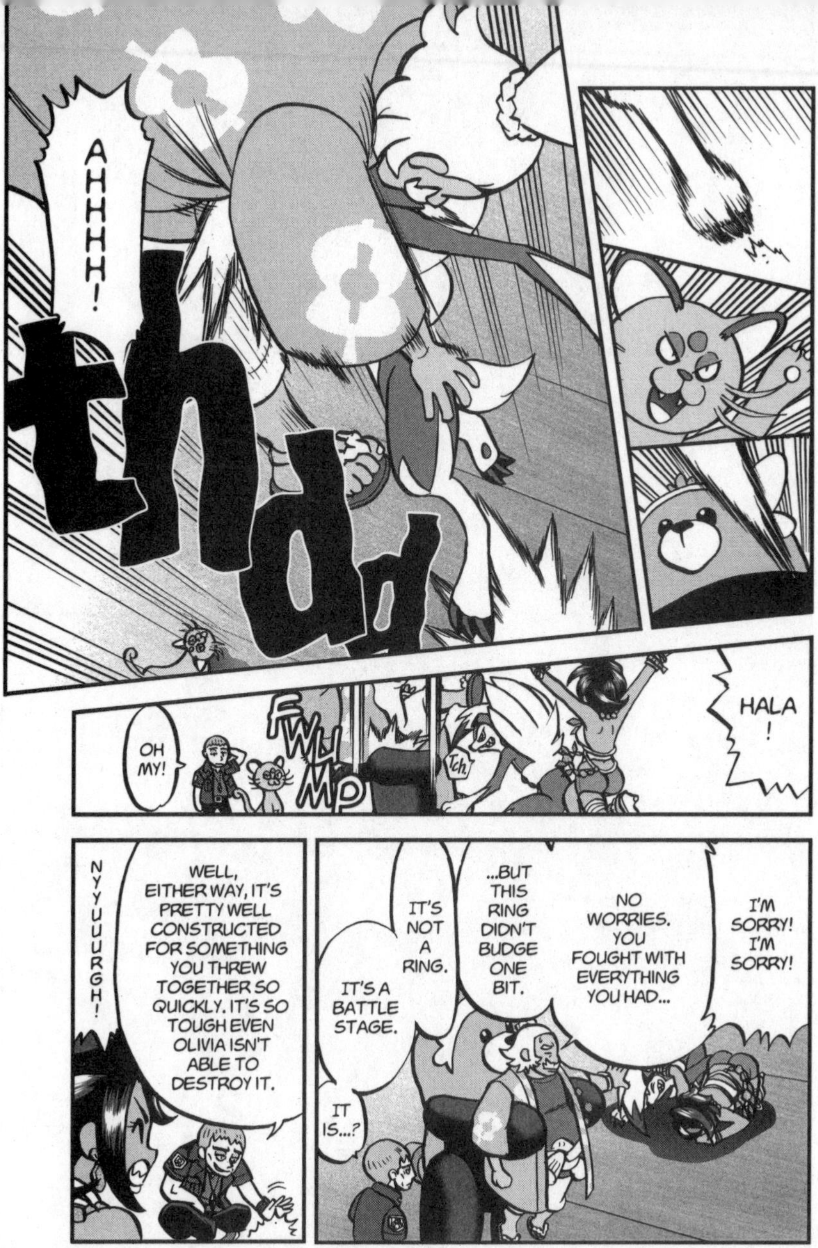
AHHHHH!
thud
HALA!
FWUMP
Tch.
OH MY!
I'M SORRY! I'M SORRY!
NO WORRIES. YOU FOUGHT WITH EVERYTHING YOU HAD...
...BUT THIS RING DIDN'T BUDGE ONE BIT.
IT'S NOT A RING.
IT'S A BATTLE STAGE.
IT IS...?
NYYUUURGH!
WELL, EITHER WAY, IT'S PRETTY WELL CONSTRUCTED FOR SOMETHING YOU THREW TOGETHER SO QUICKLY. IT'S SO TOUGH EVEN OLIVIA ISN'T ABLE TO DESTROY IT.

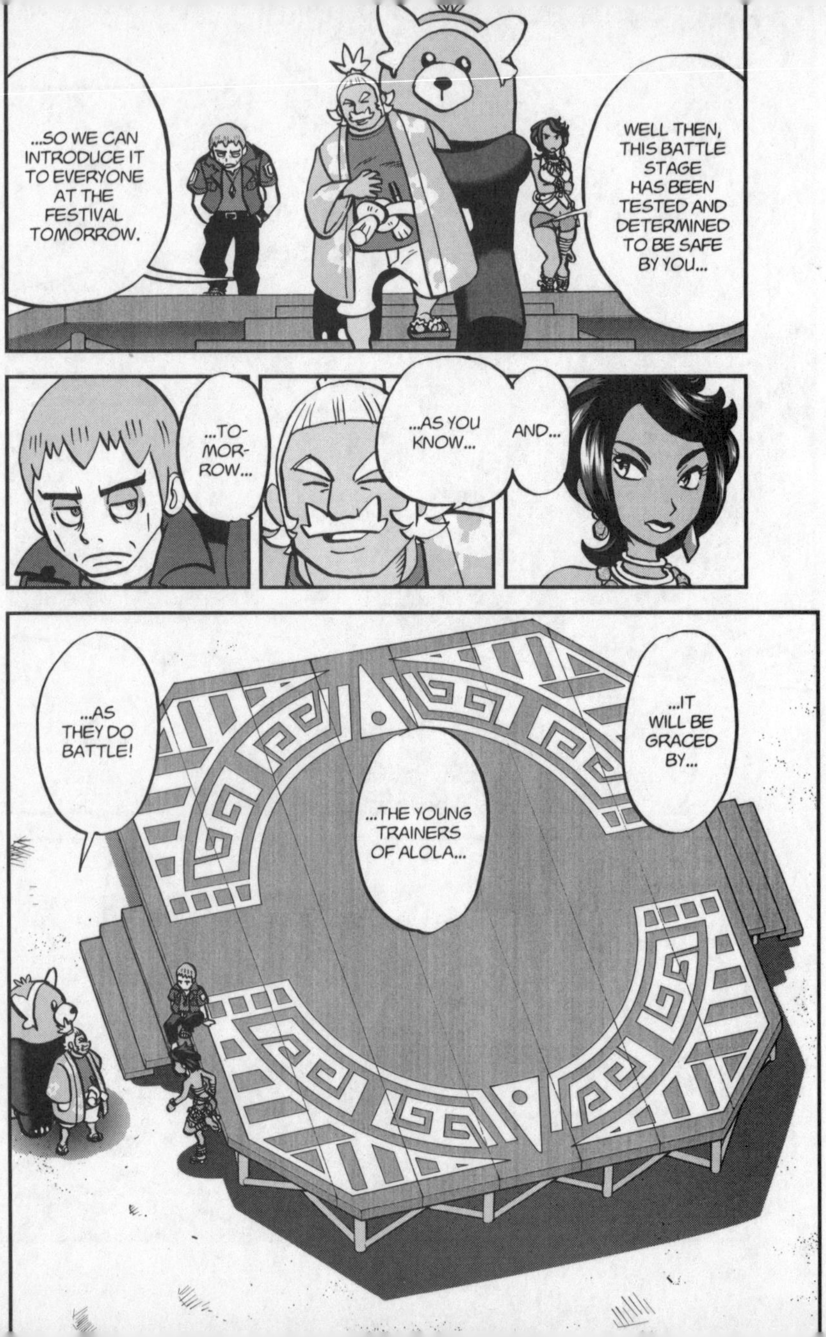
WELL THEN, THIS BATTLE STAGE HAS BEEN TESTED AND DETERMINED TO BE SAFE BY YOU...
...SO WE CAN INTRODUCE IT TO EVERYONE AT THE FESTIVAL TOMORROW.
AND...
...AS YOU KNOW...
...TO-MOR-ROW...
...IT WILL BE GRACED BY...
...THE YOUNG TRAINERS OF ALOLA...
...AS THEY DO BATTLE!

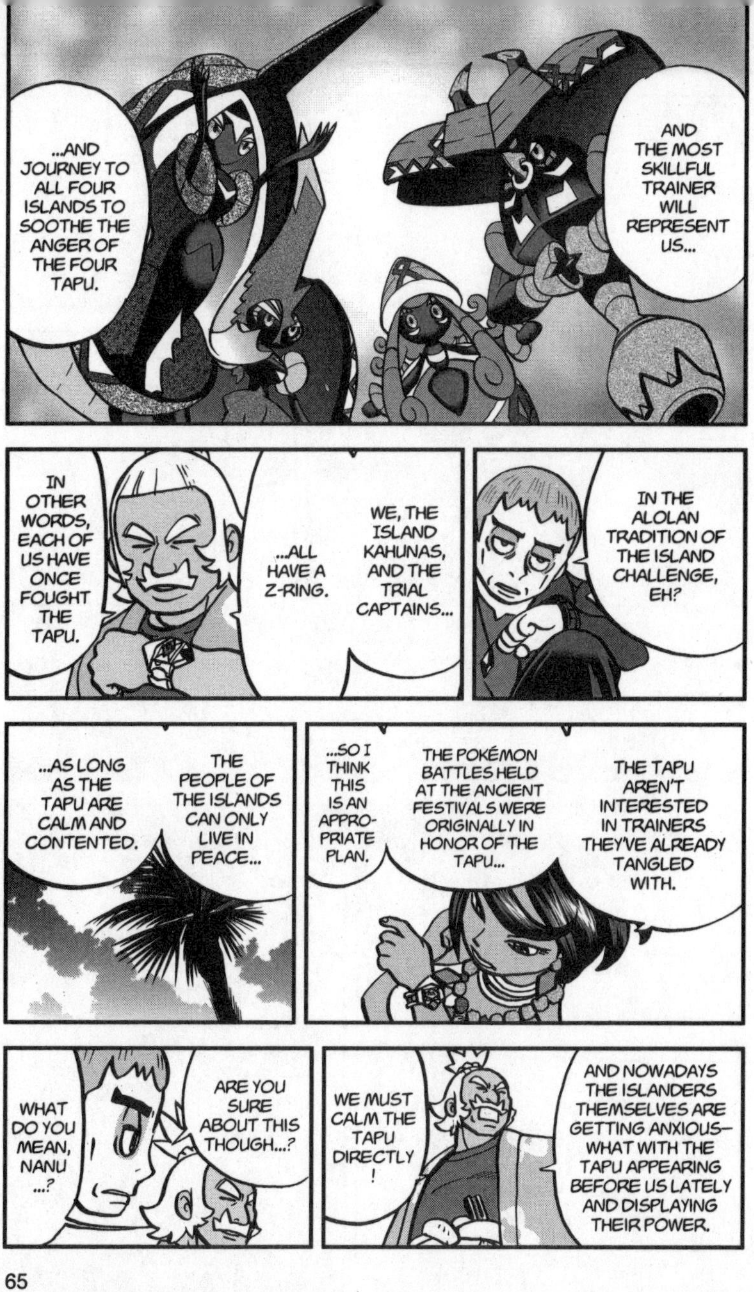
AND THE MOST SKILLFUL TRAINER WILL REPRESENT US...
...AND JOURNEY TO ALL FOUR ISLANDS TO SOOTHE THE ANGER OF THE FOUR TAPU.
IN THE ALOLAN TRADITION OF THE ISLAND CHALLENGE, EH?
WE, THE ISLAND KAHUNAS, AND THE TRIAL CAPTAINS...
...ALL HAVE A Z-RING.
IN OTHER WORDS, EACH OF US HAVE ONCE FOUGHT THE TAPU.
THE TAPU AREN'T INTERESTED IN TRAINERS THEY'VE ALREADY TANGLED WITH.
THE POKÉMON BATTLES HELD AT THE ANCIENT FESTIVALS WERE ORIGINALLY IN HONOR OF THE TAPU...
...SO I THINK THIS IS AN APPROPRIATE PLAN.
THE PEOPLE OF THE ISLANDS CAN ONLY LIVE IN PEACE...
...AS LONG AS THE TAPU ARE CALM AND CONTENTED.
AND NOWADAYS THE ISLANDERS THEMSELVES ARE GETTING ANXIOUS—WHAT WITH THE TAPU APPEARING BEFORE US LATELY AND DISPLAYING THEIR POWER.
WE MUST CALM THE TAPU DIRECTLY!
ARE YOU SURE ABOUT THIS THOUGH...?
WHAT DO YOU MEAN, NANU...?

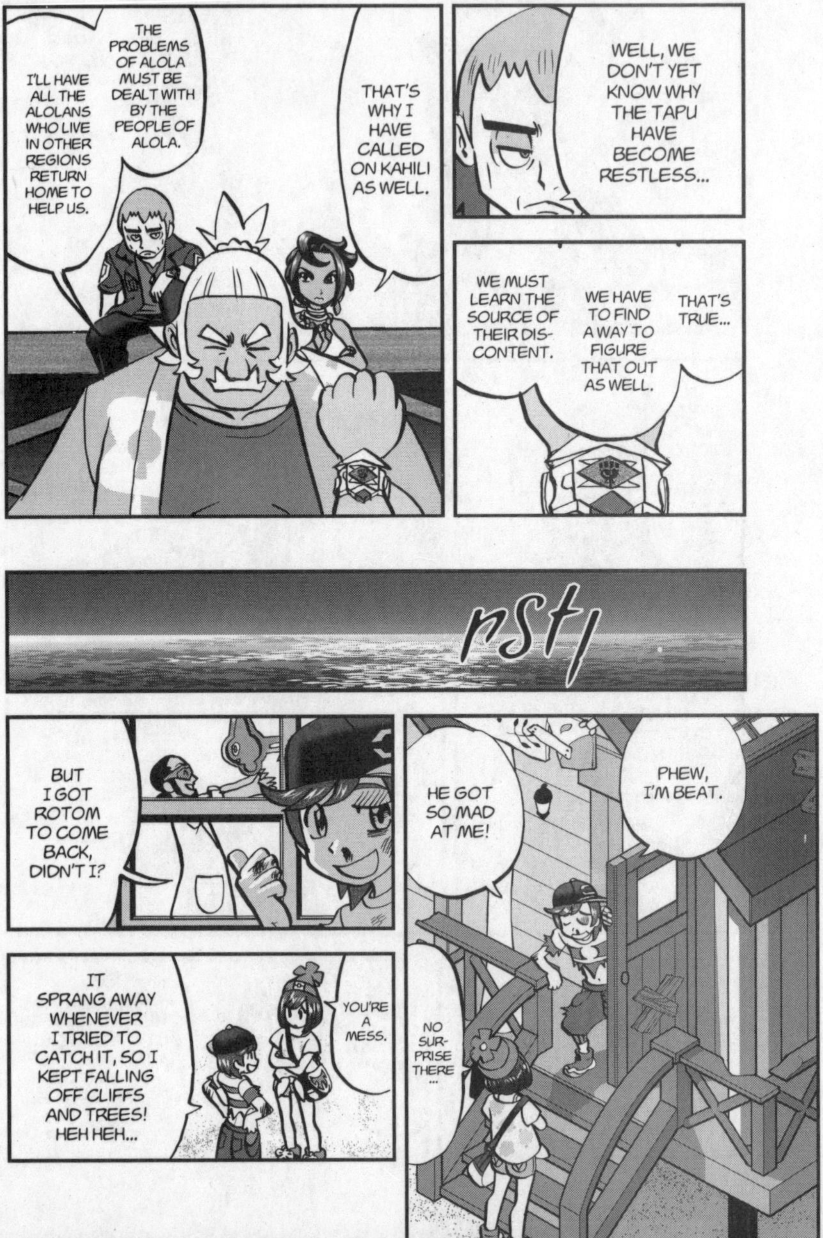
WELL, WE DON'T YET KNOW WHY THE TAPU HAVE BECOME RESTLESS...
THAT'S TRUE...
WE HAVE TO FIND A WAY TO FIGURE THAT OUT AS WELL.
WE MUST LEARN THE SOURCE OF THEIR DIS-CONTENT.
THAT'S WHY I HAVE CALLED ON KAHILI AS WELL.
THE PROBLEMS OF ALOLA MUST BE DEALT WITH BY THE PEOPLE OF ALOLA.
I'LL HAVE ALL THE ALOLANS WHO LIVE IN OTHER REGIONS RETURN HOME TO HELP US.
rstl
PHEW, I'M BEAT.
HE GOT SO MAD AT ME!
NO SUR-PRISE THERE ...
BUT I GOT ROTOM TO COME BACK, DIDN'T I?
YOU'RE A MESS.
IT SPRANG AWAY WHENEVER I TRIED TO CATCH IT, SO I KEPT FALLING OFF CLIFFS AND TREES! HEH HEH...

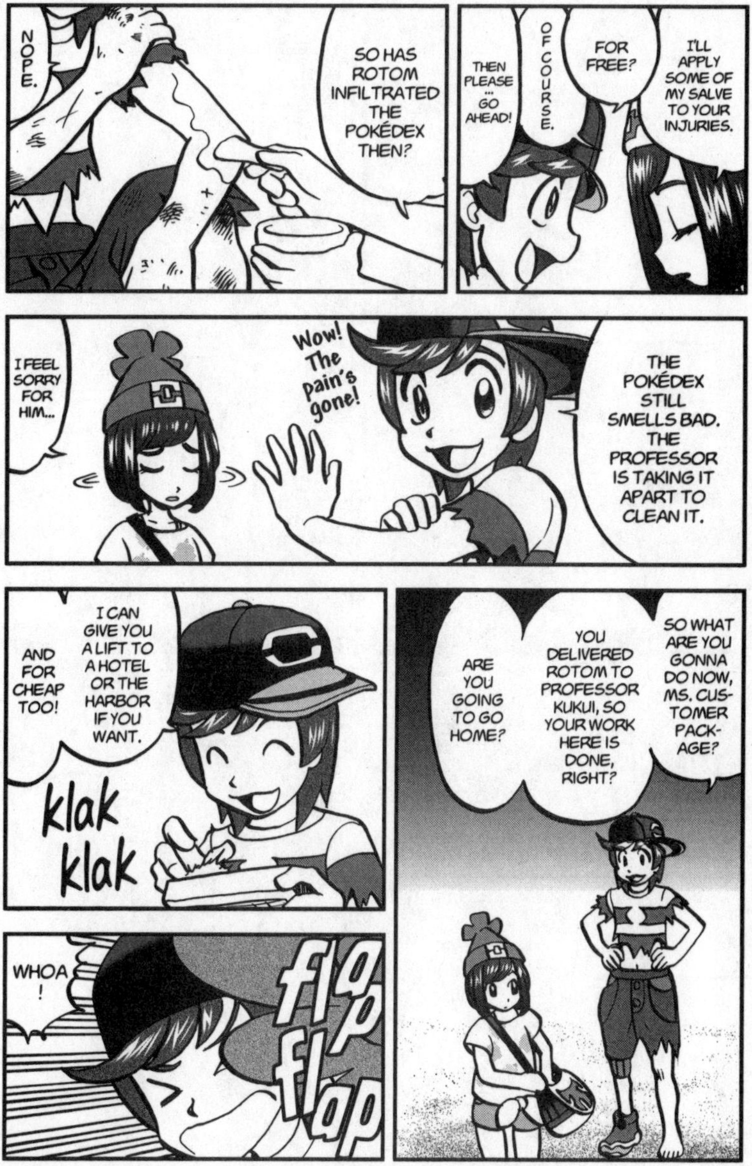
I'LL APPLY SOME OF MY SALVE TO YOUR INJURIES.
FOR FREE?
OF COURSE.
THEN PLEASE... GO AHEAD!
SO HAS ROTOM INFILTRATED THE POKÉDEX THEN?
NOPE.
THE POKÉDEX STILL SMELLS BAD. THE PROFESSOR IS TAKING IT APART TO CLEAN IT.
Wow! The pain's gone!
I FEEL SORRY FOR HIM...
SO WHAT ARE YOU GONNA DO NOW, MS. CUSTOMER PACKAGE?
YOU DELIVERED ROTOM TO PROFESSOR KUKUI, SO YOUR WORK HERE IS DONE, RIGHT?
ARE YOU GOING TO GO HOME?
I CAN GIVE YOU A LIFT TO A HOTEL OR THE HARBOR IF YOU WANT.
AND FOR CHEAP TOO!
klak klak
flap flap
WHOA!

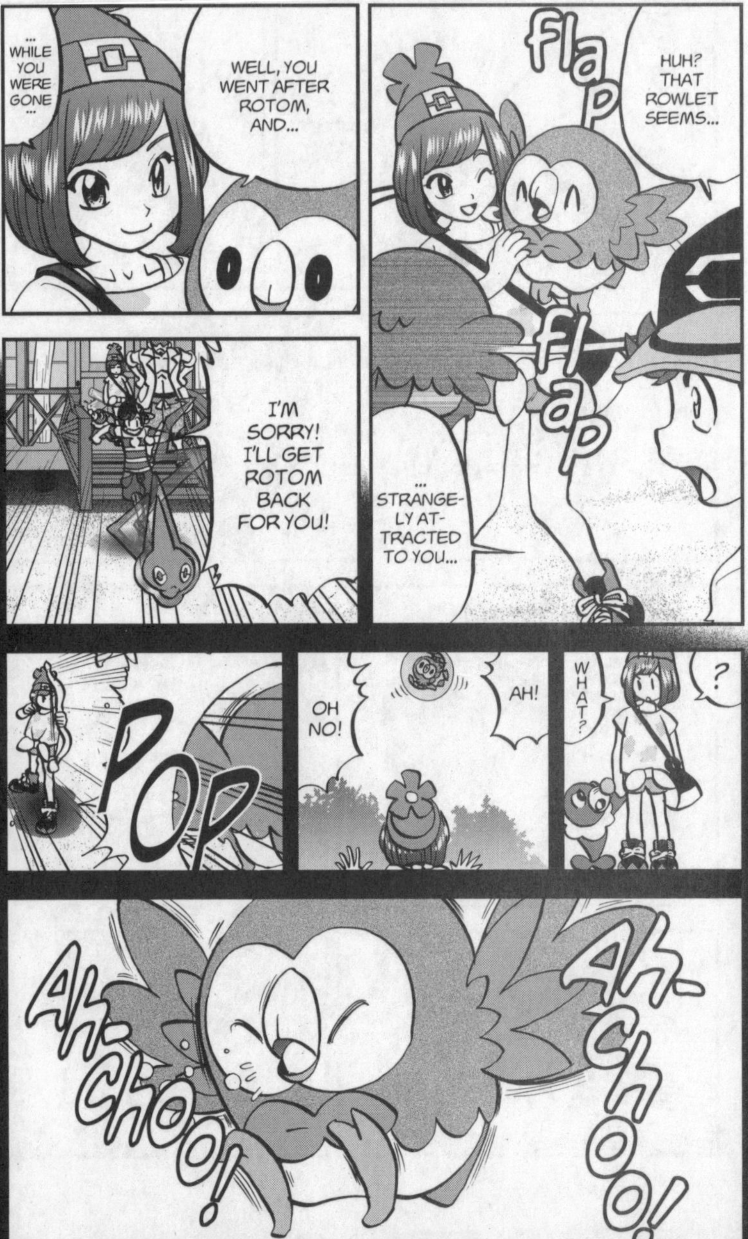
flap
HUH? THAT ROWLET SEEMS...
flap flap
...STRANGELY ATTRACTED TO YOU...
WELL, YOU WENT AFTER ROTOM, AND...
...WHILE YOU WERE GONE...
I'M SORRY! I'LL GET ROTOM BACK FOR YOU!
?
WHAT?
AH!
OH NO!
POP
Ah-choo!
Ah-choo!

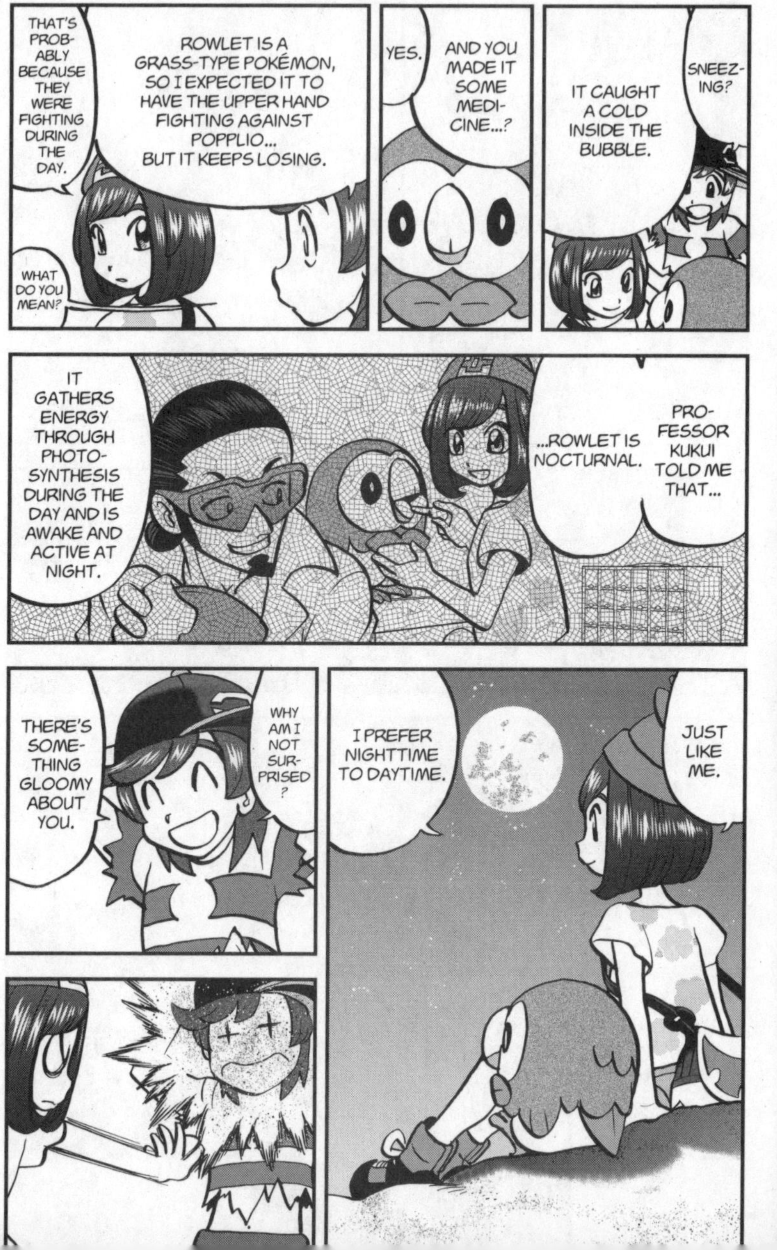
SNEEZ-ING?
IT CAUGHT A COLD INSIDE THE BUBBLE.
AND YOU MADE IT SOME MEDI-CINE...?
YES.
ROWLET IS A GRASS-TYPE POKÉMON, SO I EXPECTED IT TO HAVE THE UPPER HAND FIGHTING AGAINST POPPLIO... BUT IT KEEPS LOSING.
THAT'S PROB-ABLY BECAUSE THEY WERE FIGHTING DURING THE DAY.
WHAT DO YOU MEAN?
PRO-FESSOR KUKUI TOLD ME THAT...
...ROWLET IS NOCTURNAL.
IT GATHERS ENERGY THROUGH PHOTO-SYNTHESIS DURING THE DAY AND IS AWAKE AND ACTIVE AT NIGHT.
JUST LIKE ME.
I PREFER NIGHTTIME TO DAYTIME.
WHY AM I NOT SUR-PRISED?
THERE'S SOME-THING GLOOMY ABOUT YOU.

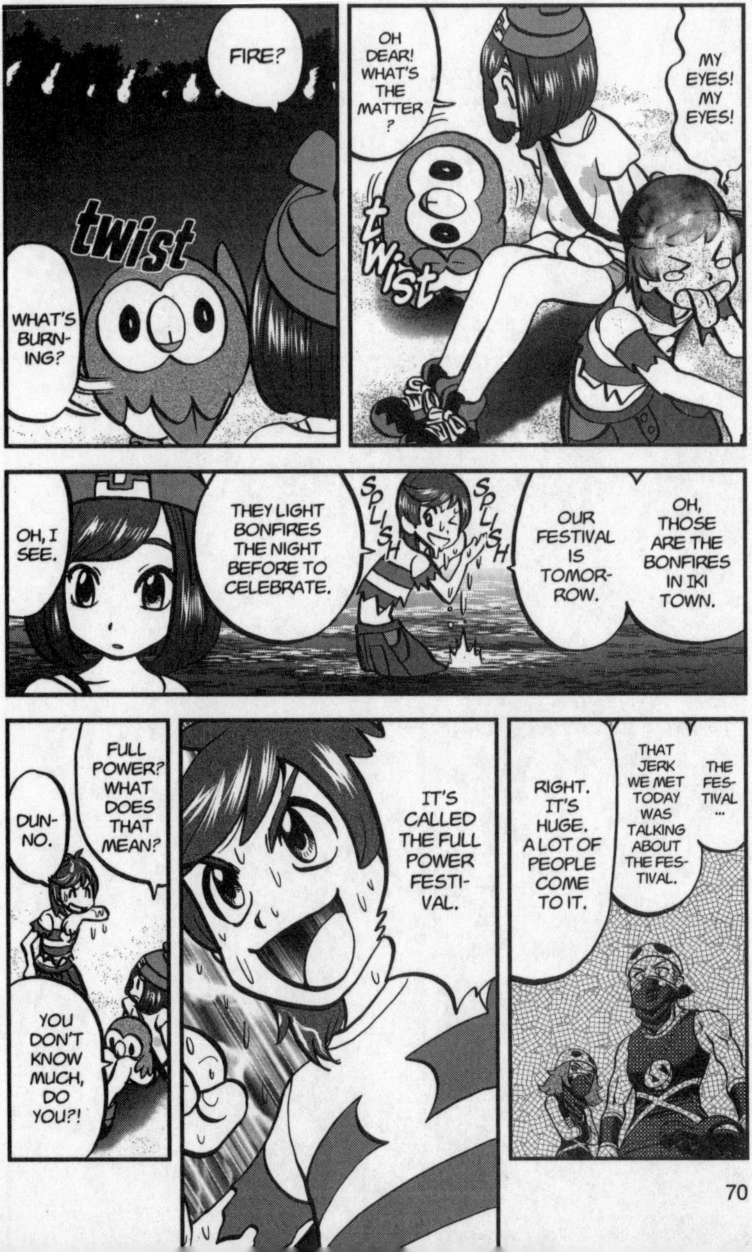
MY EYES! MY EYES!
OH DEAR! WHAT'S THE MATTER?
twist
FIRE?
twist
WHAT'S BURNING?
OH, THOSE ARE THE BONFIRES IN IKI TOWN.
OUR FESTIVAL IS TOMORROW.
SPLISH
SPLISH
THEY LIGHT BONFIRES THE NIGHT BEFORE TO CELEBRATE.
OH, I SEE.
THE FESTIVAL...
THAT JERK WE MET TODAY WAS TALKING ABOUT THE FESTIVAL.
RIGHT. IT'S HUGE. A LOT OF PEOPLE COME TO IT.
IT'S CALLED THE FULL POWER FESTIVAL.
FULL POWER? WHAT DOES THAT MEAN?
DUNNO.
YOU DON'T KNOW MUCH, DO YOU?!

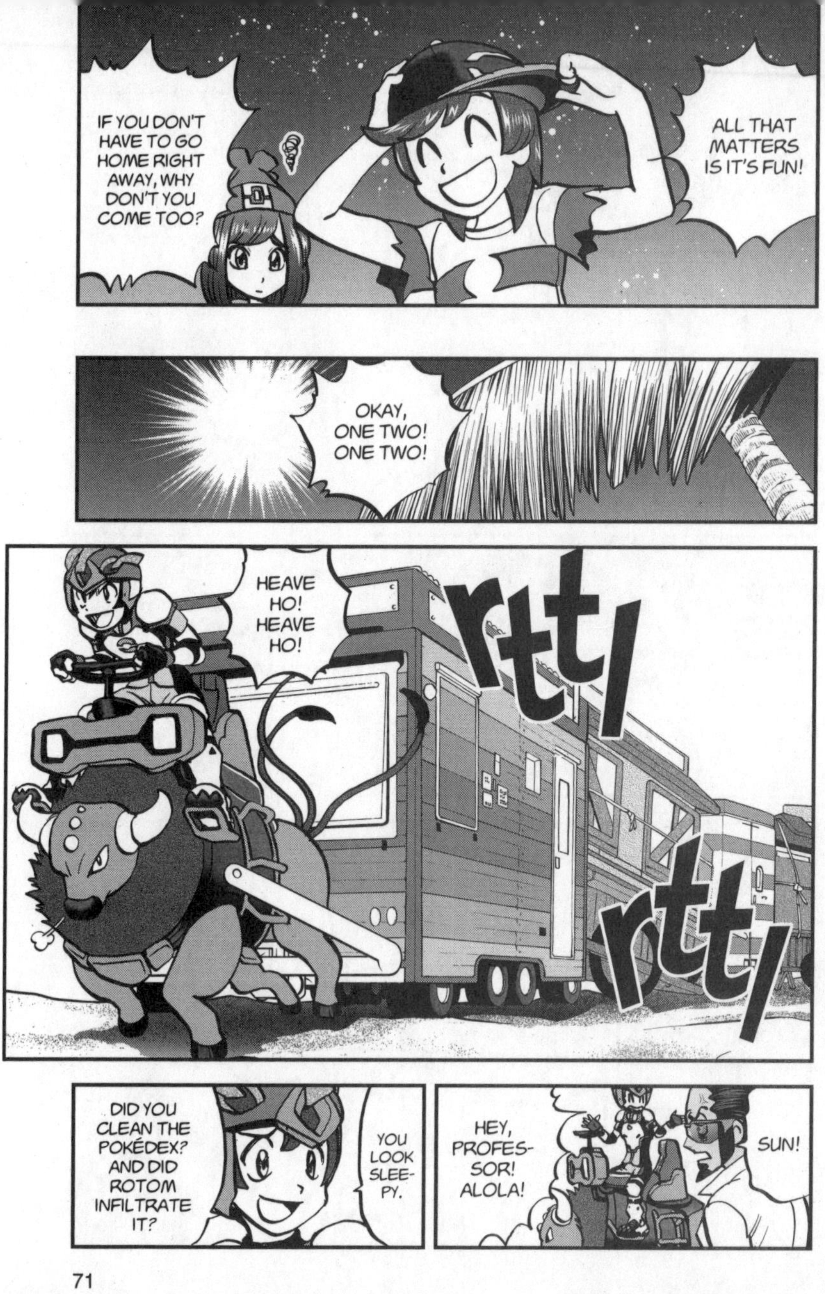
ALL THAT MATTERS IS IT'S FUN!
IF YOU DON'T HAVE TO GO HOME RIGHT AWAY, WHY DON'T YOU COME TOO?
OKAY, ONE TWO! ONE TWO!
HEAVE HO! HEAVE HO!
SUN!
HEY, PROFES-SOR! ALOLA!
YOU LOOK SLEE-PY.
DID YOU CLEAN THE POKÉDEX? AND DID ROTOM INFILTRATE IT?

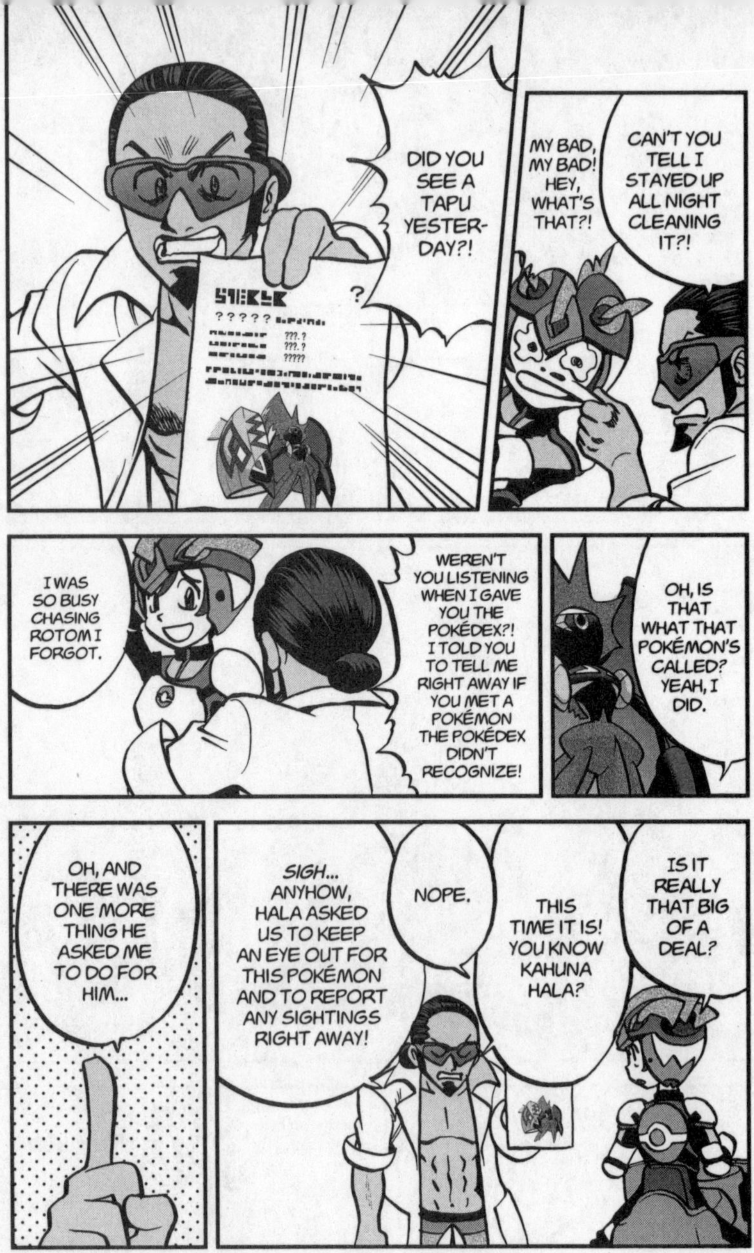
CAN'T YOU TELL I STAYED UP ALL NIGHT CLEANING IT?!
MY BAD, MY BAD! HEY, WHAT'S THAT?!
DID YOU SEE A TAPU YESTER-DAY?!
OH, IS THAT WHAT THAT POKÉMON'S CALLED? YEAH, I DID.
WEREN'T YOU LISTENING WHEN I GAVE YOU THE POKÉDEX?! I TOLD YOU TO TELL ME RIGHT AWAY IF YOU MET A POKÉMON THE POKÉDEX DIDN'T RECOGNIZE!
I WAS SO BUSY CHASING ROTOM I FORGOT.
IS IT REALLY THAT BIG OF A DEAL?
THIS TIME IT IS! YOU KNOW KAHUNA HALA?
NOPE.
SIGH... ANYHOW, HALA ASKED US TO KEEP AN EYE OUT FOR THIS POKÉMON AND TO REPORT ANY SIGHTINGS RIGHT AWAY!
OH, AND THERE WAS ONE MORE THING HE ASKED ME TO DO FOR HIM...

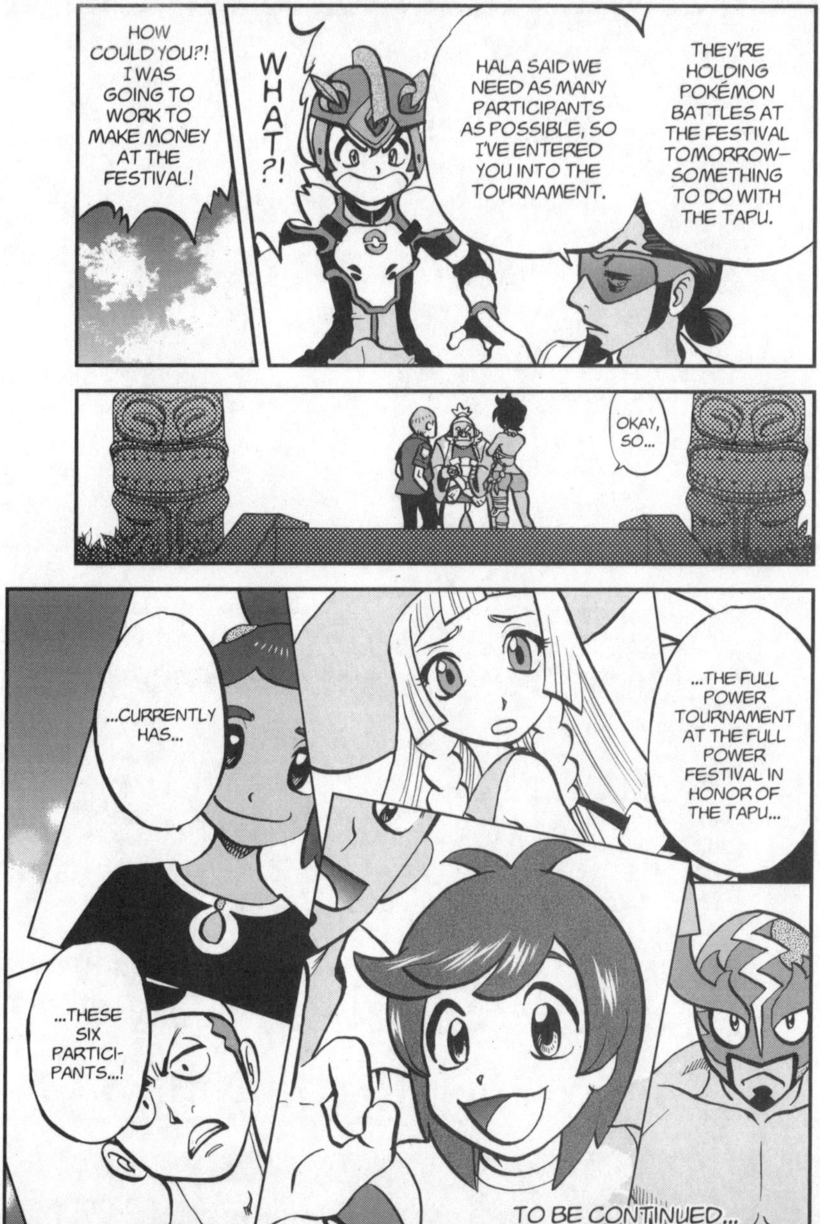
THEY'RE HOLDING POKÉMON BATTLES AT THE FESTIVAL TOMORROW—SOMETHING TO DO WITH THE TAPU.
HALA SAID WE NEED AS MANY PARTICIPANTS AS POSSIBLE, SO I'VE ENTERED YOU INTO THE TOURNAMENT.
WHAT?!
HOW COULD YOU?! I WAS GOING TO WORK TO MAKE MONEY AT THE FESTIVAL!
OKAY, SO...
...THE FULL POWER TOURNAMENT AT THE FULL POWER FESTIVAL IN HONOR OF THE TAPU...
...CURRENTLY HAS...
...THESE SIX PARTICIPANTS...!
TO BE CONTINUED...

Festival

The people of Alola hold
many outdoor festivals.
Singing and Pokémon battles
are often a part of the festivities.
The Pokémon competitions
unite everyone. ♪

Guide to Alola 3

**Pokémon Sun & Moon
Volume 1
VIZ Media Edition**

Story by HIDENORI KUSAKA
Art by SATOSHI YAMAMOTO

©2018 Pokémon.
©1995–2017 Nintendo / Creatures Inc. / GAME FREAK inc.
TM, ®, and character names are trademarks of Nintendo.
© 2017 Hidenori KUSAKA, Satoshi YAMAMOTO
All rights reserved.
Original Japanese edition published by SHOGAKUKAN.
English translation rights in the United States of America, Canada, the United Kingdom,
Ireland, Australia, New Zealand and India arranged with SHOGAKUKAN.

Original Cover Design—Hiroyuki KAWASOME (grafio)

English Adaptation—Bryant Turnage
Translation—Tetsuichiro Miyaki
Touch-Up & Lettering—Susan Daigle-Leach
Design—Alice Lewis
Editor—Annette Roman

Printed in the U.S.A.

Published by
VIZ Media, LLC
P.O. Box 77010
San Francisco, CA 94107

10 9 8 7 6
First printing, May 2018
Sixth printing, May 2024

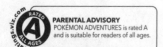

PARENTAL ADVISORY
POKÉMON ADVENTURES is rated A
and is suitable for readers of all ages.

viz.com

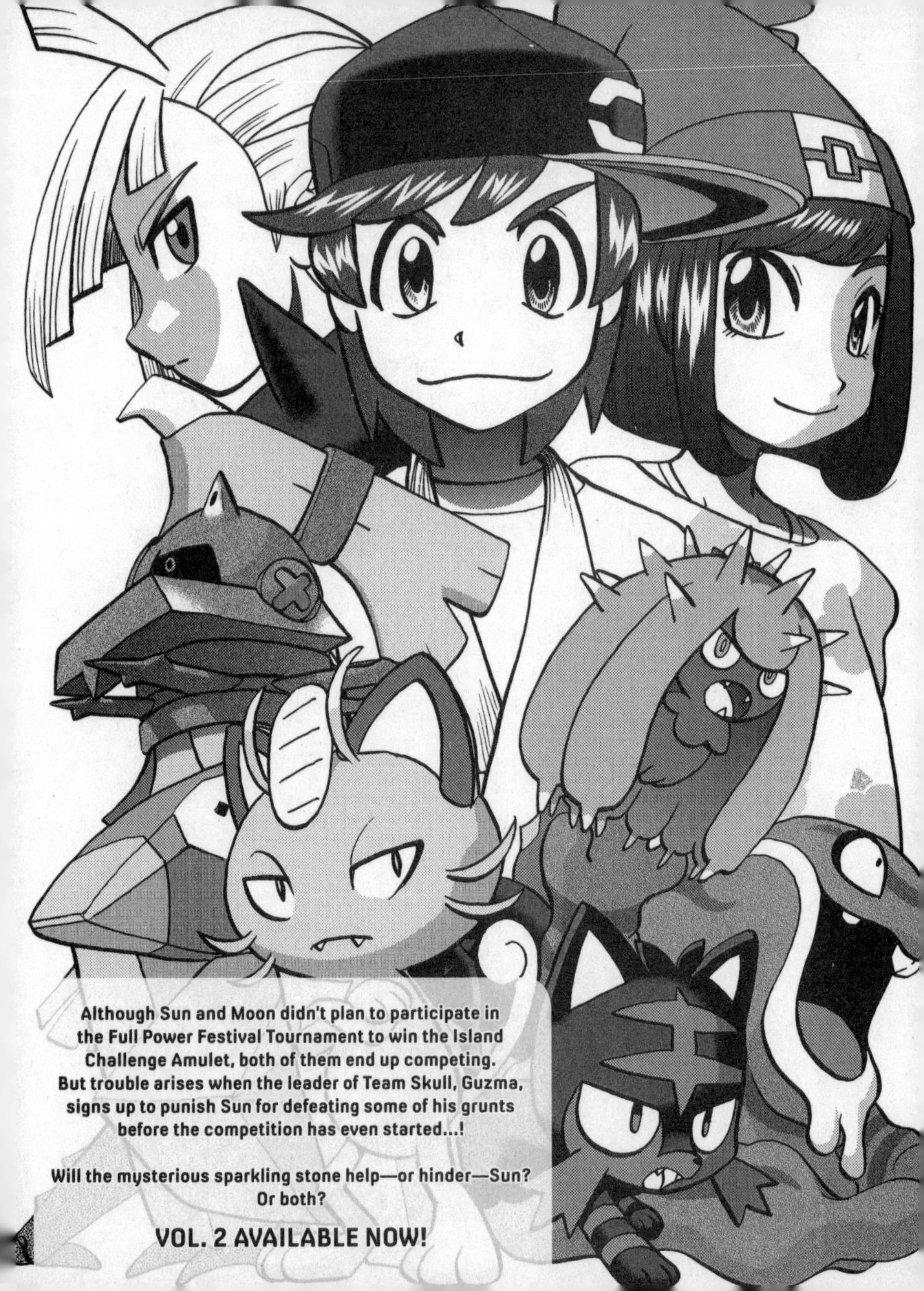
Although Sun and Moon didn't plan to participate in the Full Power Festival Tournament to win the Island Challenge Amulet, both of them end up competing. But trouble arises when the leader of Team Skull, Guzma, signs up to punish Sun for defeating some of his grunts before the competition has even started...!
Will the mysterious sparkling stone help—or hinder—Sun? Or both?
VOL. 2 AVAILABLE NOW!

POCKET COMICS

STORY & ART BY SANTA HARUKAZE

BLACK & WHITE

LEGENDARY POKÉMON

X•Y

A Pokémon pocket-sized book chock-full of four-panel gags, Pokémon trivia and fun quizzes based on the characters you know and love!

viz media
www.viz.com

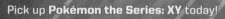

THIS IS THE END OF THIS GRAPHIC NOVEL!

To properly enjoy this VIZ Media graphic novel, please turn it around and begin reading from right to left.

This book has been printed in the original Japanese format in order to preserve the orientation of the original artwork. Have fun with it!

READ THIS WAY!

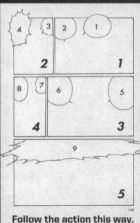

Follow the action this way.